Dragons are Forever

The Rise of the Light, Volume 4

H. M. Gooden

Published by H. M. Gooden, 2018.

DRAGONS ARE FOREVER

First edition. June 27, 2018.

Copyright © 2018 H. M. Gooden.

ISBN: 978-1775108696

Written by H. M. Gooden.

To my husband, Thomas.

You are my Jake.

Thanks for all your support,

and for giving me our little dragons.

CHAPTER ONE

The water felt soothing and cool between her toes, causing Mai to sigh. She wiggled them lazily before entering the water and transforming into a long greenish-blue shape under the bridge, safe beneath the cover of the thick fog that hid the water from prying, human eyes. She looked around in the greyness, smiling smugly as she caught sight of him. He was lying on his back, similarly relaxed and at home in the water, letting it buoy him without effort. She let her gaze follow his golden scales down, starting from the top of his beautiful head, decorated with long whiskers, all the way to his powerful hind legs. Mai felt her heart warm.

He caught her staring and quirked an elegantly shaped brow at her. "You've got a funny look on your face, love. What's going through your head?"

His deep voice sent a thrill down her spine, as it always had, and she felt the heat in her chest drop a bit lower, into her stomach. She still couldn't believe her luck, even though it had been over a year since they'd first met.

At the time, Mai had been a perpetually frightened, watery soul. She'd been completely lost in the world that she'd woken up to, after over a hundred years napping in the form of a stone dragon in a local park. But from the moment she'd seen Jake, something in her deepest being had screamed out that he was her future. No matter what the cost, she'd known she needed him in her life and then magically, he had asked her out. She was amazed that he'd felt the same way about her, although being a typical guy, he hadn't given her much in the way of sweet words or promises. Still, he treated her like gold and was great with her friends, and as Vanessa had told her more than once, that made him a keeper if ever she'd seen one.

She smiled, noticing that he was still watching her curiously, and she realized she hadn't answered. "I'm just looking at you, that's all. How did I get so lucky to meet you? With all the world and time in-between us, how did we end up together?"

Jake smiled and floated closer, putting one of his large golden claws on her smaller greenish-blue one. "It was meant to be. That's the only answer I've been able to come up with. You're from a different time and continent, so there's no way that this isn't destiny in action. Somewhere, someone wrote this in the big book of things that were supposed to happen. I, personally, have never been so grateful."

Jake stopped talking and Mai watched as he struggled to find the words, then stopped, shaking his head before looking away from her into the fog. "We should go," he said abruptly. "I think we've been here longer than we said we were going to be. Vanessa's probably waiting."

Mai went to look at her watch, then gave herself a mental smack. Duh. She didn't have a watch when she was in her dragon form. "Sure. I'm getting hungry, so you're probably right. Should we change now?"

Jake looked around, then shook his head. "Not until we get under the bridge, to the shallows. We may as well stay as warm as we can for a little while longer."

Mai inclined her head in agreement, then swam sinuously through the water, her elongated dragon's body a ripple of blue-green in the otherwise still water. She emerged smoothly in a depression where the bridge met a small green hill, before turning back into her everyday, normal human form. If anyone had been able to see her through the fog, they would have been shocked to see a brilliant azure-coloured Chinese dragon of about ten feet in length shimmer into the form of a much smaller, pretty girl of about five feet, six inches with waist length hair covering her naked body.

Luckily, but also by design, no one could see her except the man she loved. While she could have kept her clothes on throughout her shifts, she didn't enjoy wearing wet garments. Whenever she transformed near water, she made sure to tuck them away safely for afterward. They quickly dressed in clothing more appropriate for early spring in San Francisco, before joining hands and walking slowly up the small incline.

They looked like any other young couple out for a walk. He was much taller, at almost six feet, with golden brown hair and eyes and the rugged look of someone who spent a lot of time outside. She was an elegant contrast; with shiny blue-black hair, deep blue almond shaped eyes, and the regal features of ancient royalty. In San Francisco, the pairing was so commonplace that no one looked twice as they walked along the path to the parking lot. But Mai knew how unusual they really were and always worried that someone would notice and stop them. She never felt completely at ease until they were alone, so it wasn't until they got to Jake's car that she was able to let herself breathe deeply.

"Should we call her?" Jake asked, putting the car in gear and looking over his shoulder as he reversed with one hand, easily exiting the parking lot and merging with the light traffic that was Park Drive in the evening.

Mai looked at her arm, at her actual watch this time, before she grabbed her phone. "I'll text that we're on our way. It's not like we're going anywhere tonight, so I'm sure that being a little late is okay. Vanessa probably won't mind. Chances are, she's totally forgotten what time it is anyway."

Mai texted, smiling fondly as she thought about her friend. Vanessa was everything that she wasn't- outgoing, spontaneous, and vibrant. Mai often felt like a wallflower in comparison, but for some reason, Vanessa kept dragging her along, always making sure that she was included in everything. They were complete opposites in so many ways, but it seemed to work for their friendship. Mai had never had a best friend before, so she couldn't compare what was normal, but she loved her like a sister and would do anything she could for her. She looked up just in time to see the car pulling up to the three-story brownstone apartment she shared with Vanessa. It was dark inside and Mai frowned before turning to Jake.

"That's weird. None of the lights are on. Do you think she's okay? She hasn't texted yet, but that doesn't always mean anything with her."

Jake squinted, looking at the third floor windows of the apartment. "Hmm, I don't know. Things don't look unusual from here, but the lights are definitely off. Let's check it out. Maybe send her another text?"

Mai nodded, thumbs moving quickly before she undid her seatbelt and opened the door. She had a weird tickle on the back of her neck and the feeling that things weren't quite what they seemed ran through her with an irritating prickle. She didn't feel or see any signs of evil, although that wasn't really her strong suit so the absence didn't reassure her. She followed closely behind Jake, wondering if this was one of the stupid things that people did in horror movies, before mentally scolding herself.

Like she needed more to worry about!

She had her keys out between her fingers as Vanessa had taught her when she first gave them to her. A girl couldn't be too careful, she'd warned, and keys could be like knives if you used them right. Vanessa had looked gleeful that day describing the best places to put them and Mai was still surprised that she'd known as many ways to hurt people as she had.

Reaching the landing outside the apartment, Mai took a moment to listen, but heard only silence. Nothing smelled funny either, she thought as she sniffed the air, although her sense of smell as a human wasn't nearly as good as it was when she was in her dragon form. She unlocked the door and waited as Jake gestured for her to follow him, using his bulky frame to enter and block most of the doorway. She knew that he was being protective, and while Vanessa didn't like it when guys did that sort of thing for her, it made Mai feel safe when Jake did it. He took a few steps into the room and she followed carefully behind him. She wasn't sure what she was expecting, but the kitchen was quiet and the lights were out. Jake motioned her to wait before he went ahead, checking out the main living area in front of the windows, then looking into the bedrooms and bathroom before coming back and turning the light on in the kitchen.

"There's no one here but everything looks normal. I don't know where she is." Mai looked down at her phone, but it was still dark with no response to her text.

"Nothing here, either."

Mai was confused. Vanessa wasn't the most punctual person she'd ever met, but they were late, and she wasn't here or responding to her texts, which wasn't normal.

Jake leaned against the counter with his arms crossed over his chest and looked at her with concern. "Where do you think she could be?"

Mai bit her lip. It wasn't like her friend at all. "I'm not sure. Maybe she got held up on set. She was supposed to be shooting some scenes there, maybe they ran late?"

"That would explain the lack of texting too. She wouldn't be able to have her phone on her during that. Why don't we take a drive over? Check it out?" Jake suggested.

Mai agreed, feeling better with a plan. "Sure. Let me use the washroom quickly."

She crossed the living room, turning the light on in the bathroom as she closed the door. She could feel how ordinary the apartment was and wasn't sure what she'd expected to find when she'd first seen it was dark. After the last few years, with everything that had happened to her, she felt like she was always on edge. Sometimes she forgot that events could be delayed for normal reasons when she'd become used to evil soul-suckers being the cause of people acting funny or not showing up. She looked at herself in the mirror and felt a sense of disconnect.

Her face was the same as it had always been, but with a touch of makeup that no proper Chinese girl would have worn when she was a teen the first time around. Her clothes were perfectly appropriate, but still felt revealing and tight compared to what she used to wear. She looked, in fact, like every other twenty year old woman she saw in the city, even though she still felt she should be dressed in the more modest style common in the early 1900s. She only had one dress now, and that was only for special occasions, in comparison to the ankle-length dresses she'd worn every day when working in the laundry with her aunt.

She watched her face crumple at the thought of her Aunt Alice. She'd been her only remaining family after her parents had died and her loss was still fresh. It was over a hundred years ago, according to the calendar, but only months in her heart. Her aunt had taught her so much during the time they'd lived together, not quite mother-daughter, not sisters, but entwined in only the way that two lonely people can be when all your other loved ones have left you behind.

Her aunt had been her confidant, had known about her powers and tried to talk her through them, even though she hadn't had any power herself. She'd even tried to guide her in learning to control her water magic when Mai had first come into her gift. While her aunt had been able to fill in some of their families' magical history for her, it hadn't been as much as Mai had wished, although it had been more than her parents had ever told her.

Growing up, her parents had shielded her from the world of magic, afraid of the repercussions in the new world in which they lived. Racism against other humans had been so common that they didn't want to draw attention to themselves by using their supernatural gifts. Mai hadn't known anything about the fantastical world of magic and creatures until strange things had first started to happen in her early teens. Her aunt had been there for her, always supportive and loving, even while being a fierce taskmaster at the laundry that she owned.

Then the earthquake shattered everything. Mai remembered the last glimpse she'd had of her aunt, telling her to go and help others as she ran back into the business that was their livelihood. A small and determined woman, her aunt had a strength bigger than the body her spirit wore. When Mai had first woken up in San Francisco, she'd tried to find her aunt, but she'd been gone. Over one hundred years had passed. While Mai had found some evidence that she'd probably survived the earthquake and subsequent fires, record keeping during that period was spotty at best, especially for the area around Chinatown. Aunt Alice had disappeared, as so many did back then. Living lives with no documents to support they had even existed. Mai had found a bill of sale for the laundry a few years later, but it had been signed with a different name. Her aunt was long gone, but Mai missed her with a pain that was fresh.

She heard Jake call her name from the other room, a note of concern hidden in his deep tones, and she realized she'd taken way too long reminiscing.

"Coming!" Mai yelled, embarrassed by her trip to the past. She wiped away the trails left by a few errant tears that had escaped their prison. Taking a deep breath, Mai reminded herself how lucky she was. She had Vanessa and Jake, as well as other good friends in Cat, Zahara and Evelyn. She had a roof, good food, and a job to support herself honorably, even if it was in show biz. As she left the room, switching the light off behind her, she also shut off the lonely niggling feeling that even with all her blessings, without a family, she'd always be alone in the world.

CHAPTER TWO

The drive to work was short, with the girls' apartment only a five minute trip from the set. When they arrived, they noticed the parking lot was as full as it was during the day, and with relief surmised that shooting was still ongoing. They entered the door beside the craft service food tables and stood there, watching the scene that was being shot nearby. As Mai had hoped, Vanessa was there with a few of her other actor friends. Mai felt her stomach grumble and looked at the food table longingly, before she turned imploring eyes to Jake.

"I'm really hungry. Do you think you can find someone to ask how much longer this is going to be? Because this food is looking really good right now and I don't want to ruin my appetite if we're going somewhere else soon."

Jake smiled down at her and lightly grasped her chin. "Of course, my little dragon. I'd do anything for you."

He said it in a light, joking manner, but as Mai looked into his eyes and felt his hand on her face, she melted again. His eyes became molten gold as he lowered his head to give her a kiss. It was hard to stay light and Mai felt herself responding with a hunger from which they both reluctantly had to pull away. Mai backed up, breathing heavily, then looked around in embarrassment. She relaxed when she saw that no one had noticed. Jake smiled at her, then winked before going over to ask the director's assistant how things were progressing.

Mai wasn't sure how much more she could handle. She felt an overwhelming need to be with Jake at all times and fought against the strength of her attraction to him daily. He'd never pushed in any way, always staying relaxed and letting her lead the physical stage their relationship was at, but it was herself that she was worried about. This was an intensity of love that went far beyond anything she was comfortable with and she knew it had reached the point where she would consider selling her soul for him. Which was saying a lot, considering the amount of souls that she'd seen go missing over the previous few years. She couldn't imagine her life without Jake now and was finding it hard to resist taking their relationship to a more intimate level. The struggle between her feelings and her upbringing was a battle that she'd fought from the moment they'd met.

She watched him as he chatted with others, amazed by how comfortable he seemed around everyone, given his hidden differences. He was the epitome of the strong, silent type, but he also possessed a warmth that made others comfortable around him, drawing people in. She had no idea what they were talking about, but the group had grown, and several people were now laughing at something Jake had said. He had the look on his face that she'd seen when he told a joke that was a little off-color. The expression was sort of mischievous and guilty, which made him seem about seven, and was likely the reason why no one ever gave him a hard time about those jokes. The conversation continued for a few more minutes, then Jake nodded at something the director's assistant had said and walked back to her.

"He said they're on the last shot now, so Vanessa will be ready to go if she gets this take right. Sounds like she's had a rough day. Maybe we should let her pick the restaurant?"

Mai nodded. A rough day meant that the shooting hadn't gone well and Vanessa would probably be in a bad mood. Given that a bad mood from Vanessa could lead to a tornado, it was helpful to have friends with calmer constitutions nearby, in order to soothe her and keep property damage to a minimum. Food was always a great way to start, since Vanessa McLean was well known for her love of pretty much every type of cuisine.

As the two love-dragons watched, the director shouted something and people began to pack up their equipment. Mai let out a huge sigh of relief that the work day was over, but she was still starving. Hopefully, Vanessa was in the mood for something she liked.

Vanessa slumped over to them. "Hey, Mai. What's up?"

Mai smiled, patting her stomach as it chose that moment to growl. "Just hungry. But you don't really look up for going out tonight. Are you sure you still want to? We can always just grab some takeout and chill on the couch."

Mai really wanted to go out, but was concerned with how tired Vanessa seemed to be. Usually, Vanessa and Mai had more stamina than other people, since their abilities came with the perk of extra energy. Mai wondered if something else was bothering her, but didn't want to pry. Vanessa would usually let people know if she wanted any help.

"Nah, I'm fine. I'm just tired. The shoot went way over and I'm probably hypoglycemic. Anything in particular that you're in the mood for?" Vanessa stretched out her arms, doing a few side bends to get the kinks out.

Mai shook her head. "Not really, but I could eat a cow, I'm so hungry. Maybe someplace where we don't have to wait an hour for the food to get to us?"

Vanessa nodded, then snapped her fingers in an apparent moment of inspiration. "I know just the place. Jake? Do you know that Dim Sum place on Elm?"

Jake thought a moment then raised his eyebrows."Yeah, it's pretty good. Nice decor. We can get there in ten minutes, if you'd like."

Mai smiled and patted her abdomen again. "Sounds good. Well, let's go. This girl wants to eat now."

Jake smiled, giving her shoulder a quick squeeze, then they all walked off set. As promised, it was a short drive. Vanessa went in first to get seats while Jake parked, then Mai and Jake walked to the door holding hands. Jake held the door open for Mai to enter when suddenly, noise erupted all around her. Mai jumped in surprise, looking around to see not only Vanessa, but also Cat, Zahara, Evelyn, and her friends' parents. She also saw some of their friends from work. She turned to Jake in bewilderment.

He smiled and caught her chin. "Happy birthday, sweetheart."

Mai knew she looked confused. "But it's not my birthday."

Jake laughed. "I know, but since we don't really know what day that is and you haven't ever had a celebration, we decided to give you one to show you how special you are to all of us."

Mai looked around at all the smiling faces, then promptly burst into tears. Several people appeared concerned, but Cat came and gave her a hug, pulsing a little love into her aura. Mai wasn't sad, just touched, and Cat drew back with a smile.

"Just wanted to make sure that you weren't upset. We all wanted to make you feel important and loved. Hopefully it's not too much?"

Mai smiled a watery smile, luckily having just had a normal person cry, not one that would have filled the room with water. She knew that was part of the reason why Cat had come over so quickly. The first time they'd met, Mai had cried a literal river, which Cat had helped her stop by taking away some of her pain and hurt. This time it was happy tears, which Mai knew Cat could feel in her aura. It was nice, having friends like Cat, Vanessa, and Evelyn. They all had serious powers of their own, but despite that, they were still just normal people who cared about each other and those around them. While Mai had lost her entire world the day she'd turned to stone in 1906, when she'd woken up in present day San Francisco she'd gained an entirely new and rich world that helped make up for it. She felt so lucky in that moment as she looked at all the faces smiling back at her. No, she wasn't alone any more. She had family and friends, and most importantly, she had Jake. Life was pretty amazing sometimes.

"Thanks everyone, this is really lovely. I'm so grateful to have each and everyone of you here. I never thought I'd have this much love in my life. I don't have the words to express how happy I am right now. But please, can we eat? I'm starving!" Mai smiled, her tears finally dry, and everyone laughed, then sat down.

The food came quickly, as the Dim Sum carts rolled past the tables, allowing people to pick and choose the dishes that they wanted. Mai sat at the table with her friends and their parents and conversation flowed easily as always. Vanessa and Cat's mom had an art exhibition showing in Valleyview in the following month and was furiously trying to finish the last few paintings, while their dad was contentedly whiling away his time at the bank. Evelyn's mother was still employed as a nurse, but was now spending more time in administration, so she finally had fewer night shifts. Cat was ready to start as a history major at the University of San Francisco, having just graduated high school a few months earlier. She'd actually just moved on the weekend, planning to live with Vanessa and Mai. They'd already decided that the sisters would share the bigger room with two beds, while Mai would move to Vanessa's current room.

Evelyn was still something of an unknown quality. Since the events of the spring, they'd all found themselves being more careful around her. During their last adventure, Evelyn had gone from being a somewhat powerful psychic to finding out that she was a goddess and none of the girls were really sure what that meant for their friendships. Mai still liked Evelyn, and she knew that Cat and Evelyn were still best friends, but now that she was a higher being, so-to-speak, university was off the table for her. The last they'd all heard was that Evelyn planned to go her own way for a while, so the fact that she was able to come to supper made Mai even happier.

Evelyn smiled at her and Mai felt her speak inside her mind. *Are you happy?*

Mai nodded, smiling back. *I've never been happier. It's so good to see you, especially when I know how busy you must be.*

Evelyn smiled and shrugged. *I can always take the time for you guys. It's because of you that I even know who I am. The world can do for a day without me as Olukun, especially since I didn't even know that's who I was until a few months ago. What's one day compared to eighteen years?*

Mai smiled, gratitude shining from her face. *Thanks, anyway. And thanks for bringing Zahara. It's awesome she could make it.*

Mai looked at her newest friend, who'd glanced over at that moment, sensing that someone was discussing her. She waved and Mai nodded back.

"I can't believe you were able to come all the way for tonight, Zahara. That's really great." Mai spoke out loud, wanting to let Zahara know what they'd been saying.

Zahara shrugged. "Hey, any chance I get to cross the pond. I'd never ask Robin to let me use the doorways for this purpose, but if it's Evelyn's idea, then I'm all for it!"

The five girls smiled. They were sitting close enough that their regular human friends couldn't hear the conversation, but even if they had, it wouldn't have made much sense. Zahara was referring to the doorways between Summerland and the human world, which most humans didn't know existed. Since Evelyn had remembered who she was, she'd become close with Robin again. It turned out that they'd been romantic partners in her last life, and as far as Mai could tell, they'd picked right up where they'd left off. Which meant, of course, that Evelyn had access to travelling between places whenever she wanted to, and by extension, she could easily bring Zahara over from where she lived in the UK.

"How long are you staying?" Vanessa asked, raising an eyebrow.

Zahara shook her head. "I'm not really sure. It depends on Evelyn and when she wants to leave. My employer is very flexible. I took a week off, so I'm hopeful I can do a little sightseeing before I go."

Evelyn's lips curved with a Mona Lisa smile. "We can stay for a few days. I want to catch up with my bestie here and help her settle in before school starts next week. I can't believe how grown up I feel these days."

Cat gave her a sardonic eyebrow. "Dude, you are thousands of years old. I'd be surprised if you didn't feel grown up."

Evelyn snorted. "Maybe so, but I'm still in an eighteen-year-old's body. And I started out fresh when I was born. So while I may be getting back most of my memories from before, I'm still only as old as this body."

Mai looked at her curiously. "What *are* your plans for this year? I know that you aren't going to school when Cat does, but what are you going to do instead?"

Evelyn shrugged, flicking a piece of lint off her sleeve. "I'm just going to play it by ear. I'll obviously need money to live somewhere, unless I just stay in Summerland like Robin's been asking me to. But I want to learn more about my past and find out what I'm truly able to do. So I've planned a trip to Haiti with my mother to trace my family tree for the first step. We're going to leave next week. I'm not sure when we'll be back." Evelyn stopped, a twinkle in her eye as she added, "of course, we're totally flying Air Summerland. Way less expensive, and without luggage fees."

Mai smiled and shook her head. Of course. When you could travel without paying for cramped quarters, why would you ever fly? The tinkle of glass being hit with a metal utensil drew Mai's attention, and she turned find the noise being made by Jake. He stood up and the room hushed in anticipation. He looked around for a moment, his eyes shining with love as they came to rest on Mai.

"Thank you all for coming. It's amazing to see so many friends and family and I know that it means as much to Mai as it does to me that you could come tonight. Some of you have literally crossed oceans to be here. Now that I have everyone's attention, there's something I've been wanting to do for a while."

Jake turned his back to Mai for a moment, then dropped down to one knee, holding a small box in front of her. Still confused, Mai looked at the small box. It was pretty and blue, and was held open to showcase a jade and topaz Yin and Yang ring.

"Mai, I am so incredibly lucky to have you in my life. You're the best thing that's ever happened to me. Will you do me the honor of becoming my wife?"

Mai felt her ears start to hum and the rising noise in the room seemed distant, as though she was in a long tunnel. She heard a quick intake of breath from Mindy McLean, Vanessa's mother, but all she could see was Jake, kneeling in front of her with his heart in his eyes. She took his face in her hands, her heart in her eyes a perfect match to his.

"Yes."

CHAPTER THREE

M ai looked at the ring on her hand for the thousandth time since it had been placed there. It had only been a few days, but she was still having difficulty wrapping her mind around the fact that she was engaged to Jake and that they were going to get married. All of the feelings of love for him she'd had before seemed small in comparison to how she felt now. It also raised so many questions in her mind. When? Where? How? She hadn't met his family yet and she didn't have any of her own left. What would that mean for them? She almost had to sit down when the idea of children hit her. She'd never considered having kids, but if they got married, it was a real possibility. Would they even be human? What did two dragons make anyway? Luckily, just when Mai was about to hyperventilate, Cat came into the room and immediately noticed Mai wasn't herself.

"Hey, are you okay? Your aura's all messed up right now, right around the head zone." Cat waved her arm around her own head in emphasis. "Are you upset about something?"

Mai broke her focus on the ring to see Cat standing beside the doorway to her room, and looked down sheepishly. "No. I'm fine, Cat. Thanks for asking. It's just a lot to process right now. I've never been in love before and I don't have any family, so I don't know what's expected," she said, then added, "plus, dragon here. What does that mean for kids?"

Cat smiled as she came to sit next to her. "Look Mai, try not to worry. I know that's a silly thing to say, but worrying won't change anything. Whatever is meant to be will happen. You and Jake are amazing together. Anyone can see how in love you guys are. That's the most important part. Everything else is just details."

Mai sighed and tried to relax. "I know. You're right. But it's a huge step and it's happened pretty fast. Like, I'm only twenty, and here's this guy, and now we're getting married. That's a big deal."

Cat nodded sympathetically. "Well, this likely won't help with your dilemma, but have you thought about living arrangements? I mean, I know he's got a place with Dustin right now, but are you planning to move in together now that you're engaged? It wouldn't be unusual to do so. In fact, living apart is pretty rare nowadays in general. Lots of people live together for years before getting married, usually a lot older than you are, but no pressure." Cat shrugged.

Mai blushed. "I know, but I'm still a product of the time in which I was raised. I feel more comfortable living here, for now anyway. I think we'll wait until after the wedding to live as man and wife. It just doesn't feel right to me. And I know we're pretty young, but..." Mai trailed off, lost for words.

Cat put her hands up defensively. "Hey, no worries. I'm just saying it's an option. No one will judge you either way."

Mai grimaced at the idea. "I know. It's just too much change right now, I think." Mai looked at Cat curiously, changing the subject. "But what about you? Are you ready to start school?

You've only got a few days until orientation and we've still got to sort out all of your things to move in."

Cat waved her hand dismissively. "Nah, I've got this. From the sounds of it, the first week of school is mostly all about drinking and getting lost on the way to classes, so I'm not too worried. I'll have plenty of time to get settled." Seeing Mai's concern, Cat smiled. "Don't worry, little mother, that's the last thing I plan to do. I'm not even sure I can get drunk. Stupid healing abilities. On the upside, no hangovers for this girl! Ha!"

Cat laughed at her own joke while Mai watched with mild disapproval. While she did her best to be modern, she still couldn't get over the feeling that only 'bad girls' drank. Finally, Cat relented and reassured her. "I've got everything I need here already and my class schedule is ready. I'm good to go. Don't worry, I'll be totally fine."

Mai nodded, one eyebrow still raised with doubt. "Okay, if you're sure. What's Vanessa up to?"

Cat smiled, waving her hand in the direction of the door. "Oh, she's just out with our folks, letting them buy us some groceries. She's totally going to use this as a chance to get free stuff while they're out helping me move in. And Evelyn and her mom are back in Valleyview already. Apparently, they leave for their trip next Monday so they want to be packed and ready to go."

Mai was disappointed that Evelyn had left, although at least she'd had time to say goodbye to Evelyn and Zahara the day before."Well, I hope she has a good trip."

Cat gave her a half smile. "Yeah, I know. I was disappointed too. But she's got a lot going on, now that she knows her real place, and she can't always spend as much time with us as we'd like. We can still miss her though."

They shared a smile, wistfully thinking back to how Evelyn was before her awakening against the witch, Carman. Evelyn had been so different then, just a sassy teen with a boatload of confidence. Now, she was the goddess of dreams and seemed to be in a million places at once, so she was hardly ever around, and when she was, she seemed distracted all the time. They sat for a few moments quietly, enjoying sharing the silence, before they heard a soft knock on the door.

"Are you expecting someone?" Cat asked, looking toward the kitchen.

Mai looked surprised, shaking her head. "Not really, although it could be Jake. He said he'd stop by today, if he had time."

"Of course. Well, let's go and sees who it is, shall we?"

They walked over to the kitchen area, where the outside door was located. Mai opened it, happy to find her guess had been correct. Jake stood there, as handsome as always, but this time he held a bouquet of flowers in front of his chest.

"These are for you. I wanted to stop by and see how you were doing. I know the other day was kind of overwhelming for you."

Mai took the flowers, inhaling deeply. It was a simple mixed bouquet from the grocery store down the street, but the flowers smelled sweet and the look on his face was endearing. He was like a little boy, trying to please and ensure that he wasn't in trouble.

"Thanks, Jake. They're beautiful. Cat, can you grab a vase from above the fridge?"

Cat obliged, barely having to stretch with her long arm span. She took the flowers, arranging them at the sink with her back to them while her two friends hugged.

Mai looked up into Jake's worried face, giving him a quick peck of reassurance. "I'm fine, silly. Better than fine! I had an amazing man ask me to marry him. What could be bad about that?"

The corners of his mouth curved up but he still looked concerned. "Well, as long as you're sure." He paused, continuing to look uncertain before shaking his head once, like he'd decided something. "Can I ask you something?"

When Mai nodded slowly, he continued. "I know that you probably aren't ready to move in together yet, with your upbringing and all, but I don't want to be engaged for long. I love you, Mai, so much, and I want to get married as soon as possible. I know it's fast, but I'd like you to come with me to meet my family in Norway."

Mai stepped back, still holding his arm, but out of his embrace, needing some space to think. "Wow, I didn't see that coming, although I guess I should have. Well, of course I want to meet your family. When were you thinking?"

This time it was Jake that moved, beginning to pace back and forth in the kitchen, fluffing his hair absently as he scratched the back of his head. "I was thinking we could maybe go on Monday? Shooting is over for a bit and I want to get started on my life with you. Would you be ready to travel by then?"

Mai blinked then dropped down into a chair at the kitchen table. She'd thought things were moving fast before, but this put a whole new spin on the term fast. "I...guess I could be, sure.

It's not like I don't want to meet them or get started on our lives together." She looked up, speaking with more determination now. "Let's do it. Let's go to Norway on Monday." Mai faltered after saying the destination, feeling confused. "But how are we supposed to arrange a trip to Norway over the weekend? Don't we need, like a passport, or visa, or something?"

Jake scuffed his toe on his jeans, before he looked at her shyly. "I was thinking we could maybe swim there? It would be fun to travel in our true forms. We can pack a few things in a waterproof bag and buy anything else we need when we get to my parents. If that's okay with you?"

Mai felt a bubble of excitement at the idea. "I'd love that! It would be a long trip, but the idea of taking some time off to visit and be ourselves is really appealing. Let's do it!"

Jake beamed in relief before picking her up and spinning her around. Cat backed up against the counter, laughing at him. "Woah there, buddy! This is a small kitchen. Take your crazy lover's antics elsewhere please."

Jake stopped spinning Mai, shrugging at Cat. "Sorry, I got excited there for a moment. I'm going to go get my stuff ready and let Dustin know I'll be away for awhile. Pack whatever you think you'll need for the trip, just remember that you have to be able to carry it."

Mai nodded, tilting her head up to his. "See you later?"

Jake gave her a kiss. "Absolutely. I'll call you later and we can figure out the rest of the details then. I love you."

Mai smiled. "I love you too."

They hugged once more, before Jake left the two girls alone in the kitchen.

Cat arched an eyebrow. "Norway, hey? That's incredible. It's a pretty big deal to meet his parents, especially halfway around the world."

Mai felt her chest tighten, as Cat spoke the dreaded word 'parent' out loud. "Oh, God," she said. "You're right. What was I thinking? At least if they came here, I'd be on my own ground. What if they hate me?" Mai looked at Cat with desperation. "What if I hate them?"

Cat burst out laughing. "Oh, Mai. Of course they won't hate you. I don't think I've met anyone who's ever hated you. You're kind of the nicest person alive. Not to mention, I don't think anyone related to Jake would be someone you'd hate. He's the nicest guy I've ever met." Cat gave her a chiding look. "Try not to worry. Just be yourself. This will be totally fine."

Mai nodded at Cat's words, trying to take them to heart, but still felt uneasy. In her time, mothers' opinions were very important and a mother-in-law that hated you could make your life hell. She hoped Cat was right.

CHAPTER FOUR

Shortly after Jake left, Mai went to her room to pack the bare minimum of items she thought would be necessary, but found it difficult. What did you pack to meet your soon-to-be-husband's entire family in a northern country in the fall? Sweaters? Nice clothes? Gifts? She stood in front of her closet for several minutes before mentally shrugging. I should be myself, like Cat said. And that meant jeans and t-shirts and definitely sweaters if it was cold. She managed to fit everything into a sturdy waterproof backpack she thought she could still carry as a dragon, then Mai went out to find Cat and Vanessa to discuss the trip. She found them sitting in front of the TV watching Netflix, but she knew they'd been discussing her and Jake by the guilty looks the sisters exchanged. Mai sat down beside Vanessa, who turned to her, eyes bright with questions.

"So, what's the plan? Cat says you guys are going to leave Monday?" Vanessa turned the TV to a music channel and Mai saw that in addition to her curiously she seemed strangely resigned.

"Yes, I guess so. I'm excited, but things are going so fast right now I don't know what the whole plan is. I guess I'll try to make sure my bag is really waterproof. Then it sounds like we'll hit the coast and swim to Norway. I'm guessing through the northern passage, to save time."

Cat shuddered. As a creature of the fire element, she wasn't fond of anything even remotely connected to winter or cold weather. "That sounds horrible!" Cat muttered, causing Mai to smile.

"Yes, I guess it would sound awful to a phoenix, but I'm rather more insulated as a dragon. I don't notice the cold as much in that form. I figure it'll take a few days to get there, then the part that I'm actually afraid of will start."

Vanessa nodded wisely. "Meeting the in-laws."

Mai sighed, dropping her shoulders glumly. "I haven't had family in so long that I'm not sure what to expect. I mean, what if I horribly embarrass myself? What if they hate me? What's a Norwegian mother-in-law like? I know that traditional Chinese ones can be difficult, but I know almost nothing about Jake's people. I mean, he's told me a few things, and I know he was raised knowing all about his dragon heritage, but it's not something we got into too deeply," Mai smiled ruefully. "I'm not sure if you noticed or not, but he's not always the chattiest of guys."

Cat and Vanessa both snorted.

"I had no idea," Vanessa drawled, sarcastically. "Changing subjects though, do you think that you'll be back anytime soon? I mean, not to push you out or anything, but if you're going to be away for like a month, can we just leave the rooms the way they are? I mean, if I don't have to share with Cat, I'm cool with that."

Mai thought briefly. "Oh, of course! Don't worry about me. Keep your things in your room and Cat can just use mine. We can figure the rest out when I get back."

Cat smiled in relief. "Cool. I was sort of hoping you'd say that. Not that we won't miss you!" Cat rushed to add, looking stricken.

Mai laughed. "I know what you mean, don't worry. There are going to be big changes in my life over the next little while, so you guys do what you need to and I'll let you know what I'm doing as soon as I know, okay?"

Vanessa and Cat nodded.

"Deal."

MONDAY ARRIVED QUICKLY, following a whirlwind of arranging all the last-minute details. Mai had to make sure she wasn't forgetting to tie up loose ends at work, packing the required identification papers, just in case they were needed, and make sure her bag was completely waterproof. Each was a small thing, but could turn into a big problem if neglected. She also spent time with her friends, catching up and saying goodbye to everyone. Jake was around most of the time, but he also had his own details to sort out. Dustin was okay with the situation, but had already been resigned to the fact that he'd be losing his roommate sooner or later anyways with the change in their relationship status. Jake had given him his blessing to get a new roommate, if the right one came along.

Work had been a little more difficult, in the sense that it was possible that they wouldn't have jobs to come back to if they stayed away too long. Out of sight, out of mind in the film industry, after all. It wasn't a big deal to Jake, as he'd never cared about being famous, but it did bother Mai. Money was important to live on and if neither of them had a steady job, she was nervous about what they'd do for cash when they came back. Jake tried to reassure her, reminding her that they had other options and didn't need much money to live. Vanessa had chimed in as well, reminding Mai that they could always crash with them until something turned up. Slightly reassured, Mai had taken a few deep breaths and tried not to think about it. After all, they'd be away for a month, maybe more, so it wasn't something that she needed to worry about now. She could figure it out closer to when they got back, if they didn't have anything by then.

The day dawned misty and grey, as it so often did next to their part of the Pacific Ocean. Vanessa and Cat had driven Mai and Jake to the park by the bridge, so they didn't have to carry their bags the few extra blocks. Mai looked around the familiar area and her heart squeezed. This was all she'd known for so long and she didn't know what life would be like without it. It was scary to be leaving her home and she could already feel how much she'd miss it. It felt like an ending instead of a beginning. This was the last time she'd be here as a single girl, she knew it. Whatever may happen while they were away, she would return a different person. Her world was about to change in big ways, which made the moment bittersweet.

Vanessa came over, giving her a hug, almost cracking Mai's back. "Be careful over there, okay? I'm going to miss you in the apartment, especially your cooking and cleaning. And don't worry about Jake's family. I'm sure they'll love you as much as he does, well, as much as I do, anyways. I don't think anyone could love you as much as Jake does." Vanessa smiled at Jake. "Send us some postcards," she added. "If you get a chance." Vanessa backed away, looking tearful.

Mai smiled with tears in her own eyes. "Of course. As soon as we get there, I'll mail you one. Also, I'll send a text if that's okay with you. It may get here a little quicker."

Vanessa laughed and agreed. "A text is good too."

Cat stepped forward.

"Have a great trip. I know things are going to work out great. You guys are perfect for each other and his family will easily be able to see that. Definitely send me a postcard. I'm very jealous you're going to be on a trip while I'm stuck going back to school."

Mai gave her a crooked smiled. "You'll love it, I know it. The truth is, I'm a little jealous of you going to university. If things go smoothly on the trip, maybe I'll come home and register for the winter semester."

Cat clapped her hands. "That would be awesome!"

Mai hugged Cat, then watched as both Vanessa and Cat hugged Jake before stepping back. They turned their backs for a moment, as Jake and Mai slipped the clothes they were wearing into their bags and transformed into dragons.

Mai cleared her throat. "We're decent now, you can turn around."

Cat and Vanessa turned to see two large dragons in front of them where Jake and Mai had been, a golden one and an azure one, smiling in the serpentine way that dragons did. The mist hid them from the outside world but wouldn't for long, so they turned to go.

"Take care. We love you guys," Vanessa said.

"We will. Talk soon." Jake echoed Vanessa's words, then they turned and walked into the waters, disappearing into the mist on the bay.

CHAPTER FIVE

The water was delicious against her scales as she swam through the water. Mai and Jake had kept to the deeper areas as they went through the bay, carefully avoiding any of the major shipping lanes while watching for other creatures that may be lurking. Since they both had an affinity for water, they were fairly confident that they wouldn't have any issues with threats other than human ones, but they still kept their eyes and ears open.

They swam for several hours, only breaking to rest when they felt hungry. At the last minute, they'd changed direction and decided to take the southerly route, as the idea of potentially getting trapped in icebergs and not being able to surface when they wanted to didn't appeal to either of them. Schools of fish with iridescent, glinting scales and various other curious creatures gave them a wide birth, unaccustomed to sharing the water with two dragons. They made extremely good time, as dragons didn't swim the way other sea creatures did. They could travel at almost supersonic speed if they wanted to and unless they slowed down to rest or to watch the scenery, they were potentially able to cover hundreds of miles an hour. They did take some breaks to enjoy the vast beauty of the vibrant ocean ecosystems though, but by the time they decided to rest for the night, they'd already reached the islands of the Bahamas.

They waited until clouds hid the moon over a small island to come ashore in pitch dark, using the cover of night to disguise the transition to human from prying eyes. Mai stretched out with a contented sigh after dressing as she looked over at her new fiancé. It was everything she'd never known she wanted. The love of her life, plus a warm sandy beach with palm trees and a star-speckled sky. Growing up, such freedom hadn't even been an option. Now, she was able to swim as fast as the speed of sound and manipulate water while swimming with deep sea fish. Life was so strange and awesome.

"Are you doing okay so far?" Jake asked, smiling as he looked at Mai relaxing on the beach.

She grinned, stretching again lazily. "Never better. Well, I could be a bit better if you come over here and snuggle with me. I'm tired and ready to go to sleep."

Jake nodded then joined her. "Sure. It's still another few days until we get there. We should conserve our energy as much as possible."

They unrolled a sleeping bag and moved slightly until they were underneath a group of palm trees with a view of the ocean, then they fell asleep in each other's arms.

Morning dawned in shades of glorious oranges and reds over the blue of the ocean and Mai awoke to the sound of birds flying overhead. She turned her head, greeted by the sight of Jake sleeping beside her. She took a moment to watch him, without him being aware. He was so handsome, she thought. Dark golden hair, just long enough to brush his cheeks while not hiding his eyes, the stubble on his face from a day without shaving giving him a more rugged, pirate-like look. He often looked younger than he really was, so the stubble both endeared him to her as well as made him seem older.

She looked down his body, sighing softly. He was so strong and she felt so safe next to him. She felt a little prickle on her neck as she surveyed him, then looked up to find him watching her, his warm golden-brown eyes twinkling with humor.

"Caught me," she whispered.

"Good morning." His deep voice was huskier than normal and Mai found herself flushing. "Do you see something you'd like?" He teased her, enjoying her steadily darkening color.

She backed away a little, looking around the semi-exposed area they'd picked for the night. "What if someone sees us? It wouldn't be good if we were caught."

Jake smiled and brushed her cheek. "Don't worry. I just want a morning kiss."

Mai relaxed and leaned over to give him a short but sweet kiss, then fell back on manners, feeling embarrassed and out of place again with her Victorian sensibilities. "Did you sleep well?"

Jake chuckled as he raised himself up on one elbow. "I did, in fact. I've always loved sleeping under the stars, especially when the weather is perfect like it was last night. How about you?"

Mai agreed. "It's the best sleep I've had in a long time, but it could be because I was with you," she said with a smile, adding, "also, swimming two thousand miles is more exhausting than I expected. Did you happen to pack any more food?"

Jake smiled and reached over to his bag, pulling out a few breakfast bars.

"It's not much, but I figured we could always stop some-where along the way if we wanted to eat something more sub-stantial, or catch some fish here and there. We aren't in a big rush. We could spend a few days having a vacation first, if you want." He shrugged, putting the decision in her corner.

Mai looked around the tropical paradise, more beautiful than any screensaver she'd ever seen, and was tempted to stay for a few days. But the idea of Jake's family intruded and her guilty conscience kicked in.

"As much as I'd love to stay here and see everything, I wouldn't feel right keeping your family waiting. I also think I'd worry about meeting them the whole time we were here and spoil our enjoyment of any vacation. Maybe we can stop on the way back."

Jake smiled and leaned over to brush his nose across hers. "We've got our entire life, so there's plenty of time to come back later. Do you want to get going now?"

Mai looked at the bar and held it up. "After I finish this. Maybe we can get there today?"

Jake shrugged. "It's a possibility, but remember, no rush. I'm just enjoying the journey."

BY THE TIME THE SUN was bright over the waves, Mai and Jake had packed all their items away and had comfortably full bellies. They slipped back into their dragon skins and dove into the water joyfully, taking a brief moment to play with a school of dolphins that had come close to shore to check things out. They kept Mai and Jake company for a while, but fell behind when they accelerated to their dragon cruising speed.

They followed the ocean currents and came up to the coast of Portugal later that night. Mai had discovered along the way that Jake was very experienced when it came to ocean travel.

Apparently, he'd been travelling the oceans for years and had been to almost every great body of water so far in his life. Sometimes with his dad, but often alone, just to explore. Prior to moving to California, Jake had been searching for his missing piece, as he'd explained during the months that they'd been together. She just hadn't realized that he literally had been searching the depths along the way. It had certainly come in handy during this trip. He knew the best places to catch an ocean current, as well as which areas to avoid. He'd even managed to show her a few interesting shipwrecks along the coast of Morocco, on the way north to Gibraltar. It had fascinated her, knowing that people had travelled the same route as her, but saddened her as well that so many had perished. History was interesting to her, perhaps more than to the average person, as she felt she'd been a part of it.

Once again, they found a quiet beach where they could spend the night along some of the most beautiful land she'd ever seen. After she got through the stress of meeting Jake's family, it would be nice to relax along a beach somewhere, Mai thought. Her world was so much wider, now that she'd discovered her affinity for water and now that Jake had shown her how far she could go with it. The world was quite literally her playground. She could swim anywhere her four legs and scales could take her.

The next day, they ran into rougher waters on their way north. They'd narrowly managed to slide through the busy shipping lanes in the English Channel when the weather suddenly turned. The season was turning into fall and storms weren't uncommon in the North Sea. They ended up going deeper to avoid the wind and rain that were making the water near the surface choppy, but as Mai was following behind Jake, she couldn't see what had made him stop abruptly in front of her. He'd slowed so quickly that she almost collided with him, then looked at her, gesturing for her to surface.

Curious as to what Jake had seen, she followed him quickly up into the wilder waters, lifting her head to look around. As she'd suspected, it was grey and blustery, with choppy waves that were easily up to ten feet high at times. She didn't feel cold in her dragon form, and due to her greater size, the waves weren't overwhelming her the way they would have if she'd been human. But the downside to the dragon form and travelling as quickly and deeply as they had been is that it was hard to talk to each other when underwater. As a result, they had to surface when one of them wanted to speak, such as now.

"We need to be really careful now, Mai. I didn't realize where we are." Jake sounded nervous, which she didn't like. He was very rarely freaked out by anything, so the fact that he wasn't his usual calm self scared her.

"Why? What is it?" Mai knew she sounded anxious, even in her dragon form, but Jake's words weren't at all reassuring.

"Have you ever heard of a kraken?" Jake's large golden eyes looked around, scanning the grey horizon as he spoke, trying to sound nonchalant but failing miserably.

Mai felt her eyes open wide and her mouth drop open before she was able to collect herself enough to respond. "I didn't think that was a real thing."

Jake grimaced then bobbed his head. "Yeah, it kind of is. And it lives out in the middle of the area that we're going to be coming to. We're already past the North Sea, and I'd totally forgotten that the sea floor between Norway and Greenland has a very old, very large creature that dwells there, that traditionally is what is called a kraken. Movies kind of describe it as a giant octopus or squid, but it's more like a crab the size of an island. It's enormous, possibly up to a mile or two across. I'm not even sure if it thinks. It stays deep below the surface until it's ready to feed, then rises up and eats everything in a ten-mile radius, sucking everything into itself like a giant black hole. We need to be ready to move if it happens to be lunch time."

Jake sighed, frustrated. "Damn it. I can't believe I forgot about it. I'm sorry Mai. I wouldn't have come this way if I'd thought about the kraken sooner. But we're already in it's territory, so going back is just as dangerous.

Mai felt her stomach become queasy, beginning to churn like the sea around her.

"How often does the kraken need to feed?"

Jake's whiskers twitched. "It's hard to say. Legends from fishermen in our area peg it at anywhere from two or three times a year, to as far apart as once a decade, but it really just depends on when it's hungry, I think."

Mai shuddered. "I hope it's not hungry. What do we do if we see it?"

Jake gave her a quick hug, caressing her scales reassuringly even as his words amplified her fear. "We swim for our lives. This isn't a creature to speak with or try to fight. We just run."

Mai nodded, taking a shaky breath. "I can do that. Is there anything else we need to do?"

Jake turned away from her and Mai watched as he looked around, scanning the water again. They'd made good time and were now coming up to the coast of Denmark.

"Let's travel a little closer to the shore and a little higher in the water. It'll slow us down a bit, but at least we'll be closer to land if we encounter the kraken."

With that thought motivating her, Mai found it was easy to continue quickly. They'd just rounded the passage between Denmark and Norway when Mai felt a rumble in the water below them. She looked at Jake with panic and his equally frightened appearance confirmed that he'd felt the disturbance as well. They swam higher in the water, moving as fast as they could.

Suddenly, the water began churning around them, as though an underwater volcano had just erupted. Mai saw a school of smaller fish flying toward them, fighting against the current while appearing to be sucked past them into an invisible vacuum. Then she felt the tug herself, as though some magnetic force field were pulling her toward it and away from the shore. A scream rose in her chest, which she managed to stifle. When Jake looked back at her and jerked his head to the right, she looked over and redoubled her efforts.

They were close to land now, but the tug had started to pull faster and stronger, and Mai felt as though she was moving in quicksand. She sent a quick pulse of her power into the water, propelling herself forward, and managed to shake off the force that had been pulling her down. In moments, she'd changed into her human shape and was sprinting up the rocky beach that had thankfully been only a few meters ahead by the time she'd used her magic. She'd never been so happy to see land as she was at that instant.

She looked to her left, relieved by the sight of Jake stumbling up the beach beside her. Finally feeling safe from the pull of the waves, she looked out toward the direction from which they'd come. There, only a few hundred meters away, she could see what appeared to be a giant island. As she watched the island with horror, it started to shake, then it began to slowly sink down as water poured off the top into the ocean around it. In a few minutes, it had completely disappeared. Mai realized that she had narrowly avoided discovering what a real kraken looked like, up close and personal. For the first time in a long while, she was very happy she wasn't in the water.

"Oh my god, Jake. That was super close. Now what do we do?" Mai kept watching the spot where the moving island had been. "Should we stay here? I have to admit I'm kind of scared to get back into the water."

Jake looked at her, still breathing fast from his exertions. He smiled crookedly, his dragon whiskers drooping in the rain.

"Well, the good news is that we're probably safe from the kraken for awhile. It's going to be a few months until that thing is hungry again. We can travel by land from now on, but it's probably also safe to head back to the water and swim the rest of the way. Up to you."

Jake waited for her answer as Mai looked at the barren landscape around them. It wasn't cold anymore and the day looked like it would be sunny, as the rain and wind had died down at some point during their frantic swim to land. She looked back out toward the water, then shuddered again. As much as she loved swimming, she didn't really feel like hopping back into the same water where an island had tried to eat her a few minutes earlier.

"Let's change into our hiking stuff and walk. I'd like to see some of the countryside. How far is our destination from here?"

Jake grabbed his bag and quickly transformed before taking his cell phone out of a waterproof case and looking at Google maps.

"We've surfaced at a good place. It's only about a day's hike to Vestbygd, which is very close to my village. We can catch a bus from there to my parent's house. So it will only take a few hours, if you're up for some rocky ground and hard walking."

Mai smiled at Jake, having changed while he was talking into her usual jeans, t-shirt, and hooded sweater.

"I had a feeling Norway may involve hiking, so I packed my best boots." She held one up for his inspection and he smiled.

"You're learning, very good. These should allow you to almost keep up with me."

He smirked at her and she whacked his arm at his patronizing tone.

"Ha! You're so funny. It's a good thing you're so cute and that I love you."

Jake made a kissy-face, then jerked away when she went to hit him again.

"Alright, alright, we can go. Got everything?"

Mai held up her backpack for his inspection before putting it back on, tightening the straps for what she was sure would be a vigorous walk. Jake loved hiking and had introduced her to the activity from their earliest dates, once the weather had warmed up enough, as they'd met in December. He'd made her go everywhere they could to indulge his passion in the area near the San Francisco. Luckily, California was a great place to take up the hobby, as the weather was usually nice and the scenery varied. Mai was pleased that all her practice meant that she was now able to keep up with him relatively well.

It didn't take long until they saw a pretty little harbor town appear in front of them. Mai looked at the colorful houses along the dock and harbor, amused by how similar they appeared to what she remembered seeing when they'd been in Scotland, hunting for Carman. People have so much in common with those who live similarly to them, even countries apart, she mused. She could see swaying fishing boats and gliding seagulls and felt as if she could have been in any port city in the world. As they came closer, she heard people going about their day and realized she couldn't understand a word they were saying. Jake, on the other hand, broke into a wide smile and Mai could see that he was excited.

"How much farther is it?" Mai asked, as they entered the town along a path by the water.

"Well, we're really close. My family lives on the outskirts of this town. Many years ago it was its own village, but I guess you could consider it the outskirts now as the two places have kind of merged over the last few decades. It's not a big town, so people from both places tend to get grouped together for population counts anyway."

Jake spotted a bus stop and they headed over. After reading the sign, he shook his head, then took his phone out and quickly punched in a number.

"Kan du komme a plukke oss opp?"

While Mai knew Jake was speaking Norwegian, she was struck by how close the sentence sounded to English. He hung up after a minute then turned back to her.

"I got a hold of my dad. Luckily, he's nearby and not tied up, so he's going to come and get us. The next bus isn't for an hour, so this will be quicker. Are you ready to meet my parents?" Jake spoke nonchalantly, but his voice broke slightly on the last word.

Mai knew he wasn't as calm as he seemed and she felt her palms get sweaty.

"I guess so."

They looked at each other without speaking for a moment, until Jake drew her into him for a hug, leaning back to look at her bravely.

"We've got this. If we can face soul stealers, witches, and demons, then we can get through this together too."

Mai rested her head against his warm chest and sighed. "I know. I just want them to like me."

Jake lifted her chin up and kissed her on the nose. "Me too sweetie, me too. But if they like you half as much as I do, you have nothing to worry about."

CHAPTER SIX

M ai turned to the sound of a man clearing his throat, looking up with embarrassment. In front of her stood a man who looked very similar to Jake, but with the addition of a few years. He had the same stocky, muscular build with dark blond hair, although there were silver sprinkles at the temples. He had a neatly trimmed beard which had mostly turned to grey and dark brown eyes with crinkles at the corner, suggesting he either smiled frequently, or had spent many years outside in the sun.

When Jake saw him, a smile split his face. Jake released Mai from his embrace and the two men hugged, giving each other manly pats to the back when they finally pulled away.

"Far, it's good to see you!"

Mai began tearing up when she saw how tight the hug was and how happy Jake looked. It was obvious that he'd missed his father and that the two men clearly had a good relationship. There was none of the awkwardness she'd often seen with family members who didn't get along. It made her heart twist a little with sadness as well, as she remembered her aunt and her parents. They hadn't been physically affectionate the way Jake's family appeared to be, but they had loved each other.

"Jake! It's good to see you as well. Did you have any troubles on the journey?"

Mai watched as his dad seemed to be looking around for their luggage, but when he didn't see any, he took Mai's backpack from her instead.

"And you must be Mai. It's very nice to meet you. You can call me Anders, if you'd like." He spoke English fluently, with only a hint of an accent.

Mai bowed respectfully.

"It's nice to meet you as well, sir."

"Anders." He gave her a chiding look, then gestured for them to follow him to the car as Jake answered his father's earlier question.

"Only a little. We got to experience the legend of the kraken. Almost got a little too close. Luckily, we were near to shore at the time."

Anders looked at him sharply.

"Seriously, Dad, we're fine. I hadn't planned to go that way but we were travelling fast and I kind of got sidetracked."

Jake looked sheepish, but his father shook his head.

"You were taught better than that, sonn. But no harm done, right? Well, get in. Your Mor is waiting for you. And your bror and søster as well."

Jake's dad opened the door to the back seat and Mai got in gratefully. While she'd been prepared to hike, the three days of physical exertion had left her feeling exhausted and she sank comfortably into the small leather-covered backseat, while Jake slid into the passenger seat beside his dad.

As Anders drove, Mai was happy to notice they drove on the same side of the road as the United States in this country.

While she'd tried not to jump when Zahara had been behind the wheel and drove off down the left side when they'd been in the UK, Mai had felt queasy each and every time. When you get used to one thing being normal, everything else feels like a car accident waiting to happen. Especially after she'd only barely gotten used to the speed that people drove in cars. It had been a big shock when she'd first encountered modern traffic in San Francisco.

Mai listened quietly as the two men spoke in a mixture of English and Norwegian. She had a hard time telling the difference at times and often had no clue as to what was being discussed as a result. She looked out the window at the scenery as they drove, realizing that Jake hadn't been exaggerating when he'd said the town was small and everything was nearby. It took them less than ten minutes to pull up outside an average looking, two-story house right at the edge of town. Mai felt her stomach lurch when they stopped and froze in her seat, waiting for someone else to make the first move.

Jake noticed her stiff expression and tried to smile reassuringly, but failed miserably in his attempt to make her relax.

"Mai, honey, are you ready? We're here."

She gave him a tight smile. "Yes, I'm good. I'll follow you."

As before, Jake's father grabbed her bag so she was left trailing behind the men, anxious and empty-handed. *Nothing to hang onto for support*, she thought morosely, when Jake again started talking animatedly with his father.

The door to the house flew open and a bullet with long blond hair flew down the steps and into Jake's arms, wrapping her legs around him as she squealed. He laughed and spun her around in response.

"Aud! It's wonderful to see you! You've grown six inches since the last time I saw you!"

As Jake put the other woman on the ground, Mai's initial jealousy was replaced by relief when she saw that she was only about sixteen, not an adult woman as she'd first thought. Mai didn't have time to say anything though, as two more people came over to hug Jake. Everyone began to talk all at once, except Mai, who stood back in a state of quiet shock.

One of the people who'd come to hug Jake was a young man who appeared to be even younger than Aud, but other person was obviously Jake's mother. She was beautiful and golden, with blond hair, blue eyes, and a regal bearing. Mai continued to stand back during the hugging and talking; not sure of her place and feeling insecure.

As things calmed down, Jake looked around to notice that Mai was still hanging back behind his dad. He grabbed her hand and pulled her closer, presenting her to his family.

"Mom, Aud, Christian, this is Mai, my fiancée. She doesn't know any Norwegian, so I hope you'll make her feel comfortable in English. It's not her first language either, so don't be shy about having an accent when you speak."

Mai smiled as much as her face would allow, but knew that it fell short of being the warm and happy smile they were probably expecting. She couldn't help it though. She felt like a rabbit under the eye of a den of foxes, unsure if they would lick her or devour her.

Jake's mother came forward, holding out her hand out for Mai to shake. Mai took it gingerly, clearing her throat before speaking.

"It's nice to meet you. Jake speaks of you often."

Jake's mother smiled at Mai guardedly, her smile not quite reaching her eyes either. "And you, as well. You may call me Astrid. We are eager to get to know the girl who has stolen our Jake. You must tell us everything about yourself."

Mai looked at Jake with a stricken expression. What was she supposed to say? How did one explain her background? She didn't want to lie, but her life story was really unbelievable. It wasn't exactly suitable for discussing at an outdoor first meeting.

Jake noticed her panicked expression and jumped in. "That would be great, but we've been walking a long way today, and swam a fair distance before that. I don't suppose you made any food? I could eat a hundred smørbrød."

His mom's smile was much warmer than the one she'd given Mai, who couldn't help but feel judged. She sighed inwardly. His mother was probably going to be a typical dragon mama and test her.

She didn't know how tough a *real* dragon mother-in-law would be, but she'd heard enough people complain about the regular kind to be on her guard. Luckily, the idea of her son being hungry spurred Astrid to shoo them all into the house.

"Yes, everyone into the house. I have made many smørbrød, as well as some warm suppe for this chilly day."

Once again, Jake and his dad carried their meager luggage, leaving Mai to awkwardly follow behind them. It was starting to feel like a habit and she didn't like it. She'd come so far over the previous few years while attempting to fit into modern society, but this tense meeting had made her feel as if she was starting all over again, fading back into the wallpaper, and she wasn't going to let herself do that. She stiffened her shoulders and raised her head, stepping inside the door.

Yet the inside of the house was warm and comfortable. Mai knew that if she'd been visiting under other circumstances, she would have felt welcome inside. The walls were a pale wood, with the kitchen painted a bright white. The stove was a big, black shiny centrepiece, with a pot on top that was bubbling, emiting delicious smells that wafted into the room. The kitchen led into the dining area, with a long table in the same light wood she'd noticed in the kitchen, and through the far archway she could see part of a comfortable appearing couch in the living room.

Aud commanded her attention the moment Mai walked in, obstructing her view of the rest of the house.

"Mai! You must come with me. I want to show you the upstairs, where our rooms are. We've done up the spare room for you. Jake will be in his old room."

Mai trailed behind the vivacious teen as they went upstairs, as Aud continued to chatter the entire way, stopping inside a pink and blue room. Aud flipped her long blond hair as she gestured excitedly around her.

"Look, here's my room. I'm right across from you, so if you need anything just knock. I've always wanted a sister!"

Mai was simultaneously amused by Aud's animated conversation while also embarrassed to find out that his family had already arranged their sleeping situation, although it made sense. On the one hand, it was a relief that she didn't have to discuss the issue with his mother, but the reality of separate rooms also made her sad. She'd become used to sleeping close to Jake during their trip and the idea of being apart from him made her feel horrible and empty. But at the same time, she wasn't ready for something as big as sharing a room at his parent's house without being married. In her day, that wouldn't make her a very decent marriage prospect. And while she wasn't sure that they'd mind, not in today's society, she still didn't want his parents thinking that she was that type of woman.

Aud, completely oblivious to Mai's inner turmoil, bounced around the room.

"I'm so excited to meet you. I always wondered what kind of girl Jake would bring home with him. And you're a dragon, too! It would have been sad if he just fell in love with a human. This way he'll continue to pass the family gifts forward."

Aud stopped walking and covered her mouth with shock. "I'm so sorry. Not that there's anything wrong with people, that isn't what I meant. I'm just happy to have a sister who understands the difficulties and the joys that come with being different."

Mai smiled, warming up to this friendly girl. She may have put her foot in her mouth, but she was open and welcoming and Mai could tell that her intentions were good. "Don't worry, I understand. I was pleasantly surprised when I found out that Jake was a dragon as well. We had a connection from the start, but that did add another layer of shared interests that was nice."

Aud relaxed, giving Mai a grin that stretched from ear to ear.

"Thanks. You're very kind. I can't wait to get to know you better! How long are you going to stay? Are you getting married soon? Do you want to have kids soon? I love babysitting!" She flushed and stopped speaking, then looked amused at herself.

"Oops. I'm sorry for all the questions. It's just that nothing exciting ever happens here. You are very exciting to me right now."

Mai laughed out loud. Aud's interest in her was like being licked by a puppy, with her excitement being left all over the place.

"No problem. I'm not sure how long we're staying. It's pretty open right now. Maybe a month? We haven't made any plans and I'm not even sure if we have jobs to go back to, so there's nothing with a deadline that we need to get home for."

Aud clapped her hands. "That's fantastic! I'll show you everything here and maybe we can even go shopping in the city!"

Mai smiled again, not sure what to say at this point, so she just nodded. Aud kept up a steady stream of conversation until they heard a knock on the door, which Aud jumped up to answer. Thankfully, it was Jake and not his parents. Mai looked at him with a slightly dazed expression and he chuckled when he saw her face.

"So, you've had a chance to meet my chatterbox sister I see. Getting to know each other?"

Aud came and gave him a big hug and launched into another story, but Jake cut her off.

"Mercy! Aud, please! Poor Mai looks completely shell-shocked. I'm not sure she's used to this much talking."

Aud looked back at Mai, scrunching her face up apologetically. "I'm sorry, I like to talk and you're a very important new person here. Maybe I got carried away."

Mai shook her head reassuringly. "Oh no, it's been lovely. Thank you for being so welcoming. I was very nervous about meeting everyone but you've made me feel very at home, thank you."

Aud beamed at her before glaring at her brother. "See? Mai likes it. It's fine."

Jake snorted. "I'm sure she does like you, silly bean, but you're also being spastic and completely overwhelming her."

Mai could tell that they were about to launch into a sibling argument, based on cues she'd picked up from hanging around Cat and Vanessa, and quickly interrupted before things escalated.

"Guys, guys, it's okay. I'm quite hungry actually. I was hoping that we could go downstairs and eat some of the food that your mother has prepared? It sounds fantastic."

Mai exhaled in relief as they took the bait and almost pushed each other for supremacy over who got to walk beside her. Jake finally fell back with a sigh, allowing Aud to link her arm through Mai's. Mai smiled at his frustration, but did find herself feeling more at home with the simple display of sibling rivalry.

THE KITCHEN SMELLED even more wonderful than it had on the way into the house. Although it only looked like soup and sandwiches, Mai could tell that everything was homemade, including the bread, and couldn't remember the last time she'd had anything so aromatic and fresh. She sat next to Jake at the long table, with Aud quickly claiming the seat to her other side. This had the consequence of providing Mai with a friendly buffer from Astrid, who was sitting at the end of the table, watching her with a cool expression.

"Did you find everything alright? Is there anything else you will need in your room?"

She spoke with one perfectly arched eyebrow and Mai wondered how she managed to look so pristine. She must be close to sixty, but she appeared ageless in her white sweater and cream slacks. Mai wouldn't even attempt to wear such colors with her unerring ability to knock coffee and food onto herself.

"Yes, thank you. Aud was very informative and has been most helpful."

Astrid nodded with satisfaction and Mai noticed that both Anders and Christian had already started to help themselves to the food without saying a word.

"Please," Astrid gestured. "Help yourself before the boys eat it all. They have big appetites, so I encourage you to take as much as you want from the start, in case there are no seconds available."

Anders smiled at his wife, then with a twinkle in his eye explained himself. "She keeps trying to encourage us to have manners, but I have so far resisted being tamed."

Christian didn't even look up from his food, but just continued eating. He seemed to be the quiet one of the family, and as Mai watched him eat, she remembered being that age. He looked to be around thirteen and awkward, with the long bony lines and unfilled muscles of early adolescence. He likely wasn't comfortable talking with strangers if he was anything like she'd been back then.

Mai smiled politely at Astrid as she took a plate and sandwich for herself.

"Thank you. This all looks wonderful. Do you need me to help with anything? I'm not sure how you like to run things in the house, but if I can be any help, please let me know."

Mai wasn't sure how one got on the good side of a mother in-law to be, but hoped that she wasn't unknowingly doing anything wrong. Astrid smiled back with the barest hint of teeth and this time, Mai thought it looked like a real smile. Or at least, it was trying to be a real one.

"Thank you. I'll be sure to let you know. Now, I'd like to hear all about your travels. Jake, did you have any problems on your journey?"

Jake looked sideways at his dad before speaking. Mai caught an almost imperceptible shake of Ander's head before Jake turned to his mother with a guileless look.

"We had a great trip, Mom. It was smooth, nothing exciting to speak of. We spent a few nights on the beaches along the way and would like to maybe go back for our honeymoon."

Astrid's attention perked up at the word honeymoon.

"So, you plan to be married quickly, ja? Are we to start planning the wedding tomorrow? We could have everything ready within two weeks, quite easily."

Astrid looked intently at Mai with cheeks that had bloomed with color and excitement. Mai felt her stomach drop and noticed Jake pale beneath his tan.

"What? Oh, um, well, we hadn't really thought that far yet."

Jake turned, looking to Mai for help. "Mai? What do you think? Should we let my mom help with the wedding planning and get married here, before we go back to San Francisco?"

Mai felt almost as surprised at Jake's questions as she had when he'd first asked her to marry him. But when she looked at him and then back to his mother, she could see that Astrid was serious. Mai examined her face more closely, and could tell that although Jake's mom was very composed, she actually seemed anxious herself. Maybe this was her attempt at making a contribution for Jake and Mai and giving her seal of approval?

Mai forced enthusiasm to the surface that she didn't feel, inwardly cursing Jake for throwing her under the bus and leaving it to her to decide in front of his family.

"Oh, Astrid! That's such a generous offer! My only concern is getting all of our friends here in time for a wedding. If we're going to plan, can we pick a day now and let everyone know? I'd be devastated if my girlfriends weren't able to make it. They are really my only family."

Astrid gave her a true smile this time, her blue eyes sparkling with a warmth she hadn't seen there before this moment, and Mai thought she seemed much kinder suddenly.

"Of course! I'll call the hall after lunch and see what's available for rent and we'll start planning based on that. How wonderful!"

With another smile of approval from Astrid, Mai saw what Aud would look like in thirty years or so, and her heart twisted in her chest. She wondered what her own mother had looked like. Did Mai resemble her, the way Aud looked like Astrid? Her memories were fuzzy now and she'd never know, as nothing remained from her life back then; no pictures, no paintings, only what she carried in her heart and her mind. But with a new sense of hope, Mai realized it was possible that she might fit into this family yet, no matter her initial reticence, and that maybe, just maybe, she'd have a mother figure again.

CHAPTER SEVEN

L unch passed smoothly from that point onward, with the men eating the majority of the food as Astrid had forewarned. Aud and Astrid had done most of the talking, but Mai felt more comfortable answering their questions now, and was able to interject on occasion with her ideas for the wedding. Jake remained quiet, listening as the women planned around him. Mai could see that he wasn't eating much. She wondered if things were moving faster than he'd wanted them to and felt a pang of worry.

But at that same moment, Jake caught her eye. She could see the love, as well as the desire that was smoldering beneath his silence, and she felt herself flush. Maybe it wasn't his nerves, but his eagerness to live together as man and wife that was causing him to eat less than normal as a result. She felt the fire that was always there when she thought of him rise up and begin a slow burn. She didn't care much about the details of the wedding. She just knew that one way or another, she wanted to be with him forever.

Somehow, Mai managed to finish her food and continue to participate in the conversation, even with the distraction that Jake was inadvertently providing. Once the food and dishes were tided and put away, Jake stood up from the table.

"I want to show Mai the town, just the two of us. It's been great seeing everyone but I think Mai could use a small break." Jake looked at Aud teasingly before he continued. "She's had a lot of questions in the last two hours and I think we could both use a walk to clear our heads."

Aud appeared disappointed, but Astrid agreed distractedly.

"Fine, that's fine. I need to make a few calls anyways." Astrid walked out of the room with an absent wave, looking for her phone.

Anders shrugged and went through the archway from the kitchen to the living room and sat down in his recliner, grabbing the remote. "Have fun. The game's about ready to start."

Christian dropped onto the couch beside his dad without a word. Mai could see that both men had already tuned out and looked at Jake questioningly. He shrugged, then opened the door for her. She followed without a word, the company they were keeping having dispersed, and for the first time since arriving in Jake's home town, they were finally alone.

"HOW ARE YOU DOING?" Jake asked her the moment they walked out of the house, waiting for her to answer while he searched her face. He knew that it was a lot to ask of anyone, meeting an entire family at once. His family was amazing, but still, they were a lot to handle. As he'd watched them interact with her in the house, he couldn't help but worry that she'd panic and run away, breaking his heart forever.

Mai reached up and gave him a light kiss, ending it before desire had a chance to leap up and overpower them.

"I'm fine, Jake. I was a little worried about you when your mother suggested we get married in a few weeks though. If you aren't ready, that's okay, I understand. We're still very young. We have lots of time to plan our lives."

Jake grabbed her suddenly, kissing her thoroughly this time, which caused fire to quickly and thoroughly explode inside him, partially with relief at her response.

"I can't wait much longer to be with you forever."

He leaned his forehead on her as he pulled back, breathing slightly fast. "I was so surprised that my mother was ready for this. I thought we'd have a harder time convincing her we should get married. To have her offer so quickly was kind of a shock. And truthfully, I wasn't scared. I was having a hard time not picturing you in my bed."

Jake turned bright red after mentioning his bed, then watched as colour rose in Mai's face as well. He was trying so, *so* very hard to be a gentleman, the way his father had raised him. They'd always danced around the subject of sex in the past, and he'd always tried to pull back just a little, to let her set the pace, then pulling back completely before things went too far. Even though her body and her dragon were willing, he'd known that her mind and her heart weren't ready to have a 'modern' relationship yet. That was part of what made her so special to him. He knew how much she wanted him and still stopped herself. And if he were honest, it was also large part of why he wanted to get married as soon as possible.

They looked at each other with a mix of love and desire, before Mai smiled, the relief and witness evident in her voice.

"We're a fine pair, aren't we? I'm actually surprised that we've been able to resist each other for this long. I mean, it's been almost a year and we've had these feelings this entire time. You are my Yang and I am your Yin. We're meant to be together, so it's no wonder we were drawn to each other. I don't care about the wedding. I'd marry you in my T-shirt and jeans under the moon tonight if I could, so why not let your mother plan it? Weddings are mostly for family anyway. The marriage is for us to enjoy forever."

Jake nodded then hugged her, a nice, full-body hug. He lingered, but sighed before finally breaking away.

"I can't wait to be married to you. Let's look around town like I said we were going to, then text Vanessa, Cat, and the others. We may not know the date yet but we might as well give them a heads up to see if they can figure out travel plans of 'an alternative' nature if needed. At least if it's on a weekend, they won't miss too much work or school."

Mai nodded hopefully. "The Summerland doorway is a very convenient mode of transportation, to be sure."

Jake remembered with optimism how quick it had been to travel back to the States from the UK the year before. Things had begun to move fast now, but it felt right, and he couldn't wait to get the wedding over with. He wasn't excited about the wedding part, but the marriage, like Mai had said. And he'd been ready for that almost from the day they'd met, so he had no doubts at all that he wanted her in his life forever.

THE TOWN WAS A BEAUTIFUL seaside settlement that felt familiar to Mai. She couldn't help but compare it to the small Scottish coastal town they'd spent time in when they'd fought off Carman the previous spring. The biggest difference she felt was the lack of darkness around them and the fact she didn't have to watch for soul suckers. It was a sunny day and the people were friendly, without any taint of darkness that she could tell. Everywhere she looked, she saw happy, average people going about their day. Occasionally, one would wave at them. Twice, she watched with amusement as men came over to give Jake a hug and a clap on the back.

She looked at Jake with curiosity and he smiled.

"It's a small town. I know these men from working summers in their fields as a teenager. I've only been away for about four years and it feels good to reconnect. It's the way life is here."

Mai shook her head with wonder at the uncomplicated response. "I'm not sure how you were ever able to tear yourself away from here. I guess after what I've been through, this place feels so much more welcoming than San Francisco. I'd give anything to have a family in a town that's friendly like this. Even growing up, I was always a little bit lonely. My parents were dead and while my aunt was wonderful, we spent our time working for, not socializing with, those in the city around us."

Jake touched her face before dropping a quick kiss on her forehead.

"I do love it here. You're right, it wasn't easy leaving, but I was young and wanted to make my way in the world, to see what else, who else, was out there."

Mai smirked at that and Jake wiggled his eyebrows in response.

"I was looking for my Yin, as you know as well. I knew that I'd never find someone here. It's too small and I literally already knew everyone. And I had some, er, specific requirements that made finding a partner even more challenging."

Mai looked at the ground, picking her steps out carefully as they crossed a rocky path over to a harbor lookout point while she formulated her response.

"So now that we've found each other and will be married soon, then what? Our lives are in San Francisco, but everyone you love is here. Life's short and as we've both already discovered, it can also be full of weirdness that makes sticking close to those you love more important. Have you ever thought of moving back?"

Mai stopped walking, turning to look at him as she waited for his response.

Jake sighed then stopped as well. They'd reached a railing along the boardwalk and he leaned on it, looking out at the vast waters for a moment before he answered.

"The ocean is in my veins, for sure, and so is this town. But San Francisco has become my home as well. The sea is still there, as are all of our friends. I'd be happy to stay there, but I think some part of me has always thought I'd come back here someday, when I was ready to settle down."

Jake looked at her with trepidation as his admission sank into the air between them, heavy with importance, and he back-pedaled. "It's not something I've thought about doing right away though. If you don't want to move, now or ever, I'm more than happy to return to San Francisco after our visit is over."

Now it was Mai's turn to look out over the water and away from Jake's worried face. She knew that her response would carry the weight of their future with it. She spoke slowly, considering what he was really asking, even though he'd tried to downplay his feelings. "Meeting your family, seeing where you grew up, I can't understand how you had the courage to leave it all behind. Of course you want to come back here. This is, and always will be, your home. We'll figure something out. Maybe this will someday be my home as well, but I do know that as long as I'm with you, I'll always feel like I'm home."

Jake gathered her into his arms and held her, tucking her head under his chin.

"We have plenty of time to decide. I'm just enjoying being here with you now. I never imagined how wonderful life could be before you came into it."

They stood silently for a few minutes, while the surf crashed below them and the plaintive complaints of gulls filled the air of the otherwise peaceful shore.

CHAPTER EIGHT

M ai enjoyed their walk around the town. Since it only had about a thousand people in it, give or take, it hadn't taken long for Jake to show her all the high points. In fact, a few times, they'd even doubled back over already covered ground, just to pass the time.

"I think I've shown you absolutely everything there is to see here. We could take a car to see some of the outskirts, but we've probably been away long enough." Jake sighed, looking at Mai with regret.

She knew that he was as reluctant to return to his parents house as she was, but she also knew he was right. "We should get back. I'm sure that your mother will have some news about our wedding plans by now. She seems very efficient." Mai glanced at Jake, catching his amused expression, before he hooted with laughter.

"You have no idea! She could have been a great military general. When I was a kid, she volunteered for every committee and ending up planning most of my school outings. I think she thrives on challenge."

Mai smiled, picturing Astrid directing troops of school children, and knew that Jake was right. She seemed like a force to be reckoned with on Mai's brief meeting with her and Mai wanted to make sure that she remained on her good side. They walked more slowly on the return trip, enjoying their last few moments of alone time. Mai knew without a doubt that Aud would be excited to see her and would likely have a million questions to ask the minute Mai set foot over the entryway, so she treasured the quiet while it lasted.

When they got back to the house though, things were silent. Christian was in the living room playing video games wearing headphones. He grunted a response when Jake put his hand on his shoulder, but continued with his game. They didn't see anyone else, so they took a seat on the couch and watched him while he continued to play.

"How's it going?" Jake asked his brother, just as his character died in the game.

Christian shrugged. "It's okay. School. You know."

Jake nodded. "Playing any sports this year?"

Christian raised a shoulder slightly and Mai noticed a countdown on for his game.

"Some hockey."

The action started again and both Christian and Jake fell silent. Mai was starting to get bored. She'd just pulled out her phone when Astrid reappeared.

"Oh, good. You're back." Astrid looked down at a stack of papers that she was carrying, then smiled back at Mai. "I was able to secure a venue and a caterer for next Saturday. I hope that will work for you?"

Mai felt her mouth drop open a few centimetres before she caught herself.

"Ummm, I think so?"

Astrid nodded brightly then checked something on a piece of paper.

Mai looked at Jake, who also seemed caught off guard, letting him ask the next question.

"Where were you able to get on such short notice?" Jake tried to keep his voice level, but they all heard it crack.

Christian snorted in the background but kept playing his game, unabashedly eavesdropping.

"The church is available that day and we can do a hand-fasting ceremony over by the sea either before or after that. There's a lovely spot your father and I used years ago. I think it's only fitting that we have some tradition included, along with the legal requirements, of course."

Astrid looked down at her paper again anxiously, before checking with Mai, who was surprised when she heard the formidable woman hesitate. "If that's alright with you? I'm not sure if there is any traditions you wish to include from your heritage?"

Mai could tell that Astrid was trying to respect her wishes in planning the wedding and her shoulders relaxed slightly.

"I don't know what they would all be. I was very young when my parents died, then I lost my aunt when I was about sixteen. The only wedding I remember attending was as a child, where the bride wearing a beautiful dress with red. At some point during the ceremony they released paper lanterns over the water. That's all I know."

Mai felt sad as she remembered that wedding. She'd been six and very excited. It had been a wedding of the daughter of one of her father's diplomatic connections and the entire event had been magical to her- especially the way the box lanterns had seemed to float into the sky like glorious angels of fire.

Jake noticed her face droop at the memory and pulled her closer to him on the couch.

"I like the idea of you wearing red. It's definitely a color that makes you even more beautiful. And lanterns would be a nice way to end the ceremony, don't you think Mom?" Jake turned back to his mom, looking eager at the idea.

She nodded. "It sounds lovely. We can do an afternoon church service, followed by a hand-fasting outside and then paper lanterns as the sun sets. Mai, you'll need to have a dress made. I know just the woman. Would you be able to meet her tomorrow? I've already spoken with her and she's available and expecting you. I want to get started on that right away, as it will most likely take the most time to prepare."

Mai nodded gratefully. "That should be fine. I don't have any other plans that I know of. Was there anything you had planned, Jake?" Mai looked at Jake.

He shook his head. "We'll make time for that. I was just going to show you some of the historical areas near town, but that can wait until afternoon. We'll go talk to the dress lady, then we can go for lunch and do some touring afterward."

As they spoke more about the arrangements for the day, Mai realized that not only was her almost mother-in-law well put together, but she was also very particular about details. While obviously trying to be flexible for the bridal couple, Mai could tell that Astrid was having a hard time remembering to ask for their opinions about what they wanted. By the end of the hour, Mai had been told where they'd be getting married, when, by whom, and what to expect for food, flowers, and guests. She'd been flooded with anxiety when she'd heard that she could expect to say her vows in front of an audience of several hundred people. She tried to calm herself by reminding herself that it was only for one day and everything that could be prepared for in advance would be done, so there was nothing to worry about, but it didn't help and she suddenly felt the need to escape.

"I'm sorry, but I'm feeling really tired. Would it be okay with you if I went to lie down?" Mai's head was swimming with details and she felt a little sick.

"Oh, of course. We can continue later. I've got a few more phone calls to make right now anyway. If you aren't down by supper time, I'll send Jake or Aud up to get you." Astrid, oblivious to Mai's turmoil, practically glowed with excitement.

Mai smiled weakly, before standing and walking up the stairs to return to the room Aud had shown her earlier. When Mai opened her door, she was so grateful to see the bed that she flopped down onto it and closed her eyes, taking several deep breaths. Her introvert senses had been completely overwhelmed.

Vows in front of the entire town?

But at the same time she felt on the verge of a panic attack, she was still looking forward to marrying Jake. She was also legitimately tired, so maybe some of her anxiety was simply due to lack of sleep. Mai closed her eyes for a minute to try to relax, but when she opened them a few moments later, she was confused to see that the light in the room had almost disappeared. Looking at her watch, she realized that she'd slept for several hours, and it was already into the evening. She felt embarrassed until she remembered that she'd asked to go lie down because she was tired. Well, at least she hadn't been lying.

Mai found her phone and quickly texted Vanessa, Cat, Zahara, and Evelyn; opening a group chat to let them know that her wedding plans were in full effect for the near future. Then she got up to check her reflection in the mirror. Satisfied that she looked slightly less pale than when she'd first come up to the room, Mai quietly opened the door and went downstairs.

The whole family, including Jake, were seated in the living room and appeared to be having a rousing game of monopoly. Jake looked up when he heard her on the stairs and came to meet her.

"Are you feeling better? I was a little worried that we'd played you out."

Mai smiled. "It's mostly the travel. I'm not used to that much exercise and needed to have a nap, but I feel fine otherwise. Much better now."

Mai tried to reassure Jake, but he kept looking at her with concern, so she continued. "I'm a little hungry though. Did I miss out on supper? I could make myself a sandwich if you show me where you keep things?"

Aud jumped up and stepped between them, pulling at Mai's hand. "Come. I'll show you where all the food is. I went upstairs to wake you for supper but when I saw you sound asleep, I didn't want to bother you. But now that you're awake, I want to talk about the wedding plans! It's so exciting!"

She continued to talk as she led Mai away, giving Mai just enough time to throw an amused glance over her shoulder at Jake who just shrugged helplessly and mouthed 'good luck'.

Mai found that Aud could prep food as fast as she spoke. Within minutes, Mai was seated at the table with another sandwich comprising of thick bread, cheese, and meat while Aud kept up the same endless stream of conversation. Mai felt her energy drain again as she finished the food and realized that she wasn't as caught up on rest as she'd thought she'd been following her nap.

"Listen, Aud, I know I just woke up, but after eating, I think I'm ready to go to bed for the night. Can we talk more tomorrow? I'm having a good time I promise but my eyes are feeling really heavy." Mai rubbed them for effect.

Aud clucked at her. "Well, of course! Let's get you up to bed again. Your day will be starting early with the wedding planning anyway. Christian and I have school, but we can talk more tomorrow night."

Mai smiled warmly at the younger woman. "Thanks for being so understanding. I'd love to chat more tomorrow."

Mai cleaned her plate up and walked back to the living room to give her regrets for bowing out so early. After a brief round of good nights from the family and a chaste hug and kiss from Jake, Mai went back to bed.

CHAPTER NINE

Mai slept deeply that night, but her dreams were troubled. All night, images of being left at the altar played through her head. Jake was standing at the end of the aisle, waiting for her, then suddenly he turned into the dark man, Dub. She screamed as soul suckers attacked the wedding, crying as Aud fell beneath one and lay still. Mai tossed and turned as the images changed to ones of Jake telling her that he didn't love her, then walking away as she cried. Then, while she died from a broken heart in her dream, she thought she heard the sound of a small child crying somewhere nearby.

She lifted fractionally from her nightmare, her conscious mind recognizing something was different about the noise. It sounded like it was in the next room, or somewhere nearby. She tried to find the child in her dream, but when she looked for them, the sound disappeared and her dreams faded away into the haziness of deep sleep.

THE SUN STREAMED ACROSS her bed, let in by lacy curtains that were never meant to block the light. Mai squeezed her eyes tighter and pulled the pillow over her head before awareness returned and she rolled back over. Slowly, she returned to her surroundings, realizing that it was already past seven. She'd slept for ten hours straight, fourteen if she included her nap preceding her supper sandwich the previous night. Mai stood cautiously, testing her body, and was happy to discover that she felt almost back to her normal self.

She dressed quickly and went downstairs to find the atmosphere at the table wasn't the comfortable one that she'd already become accustomed to during her short time at the Larsen house. Aud and Christian were there, eating breakfast before school, but appeared to be having a hard time choking down their cereal. Christian looked completely miserable, but Aud seemed pale and shaky, which surprised Mai more. Astrid and Anders were standing in the kitchen holding hands and with grim expressions, while Jake was at the table looking more upset than Mai had ever seen him. Fearing the worst, Mai announced her presence.

"Good morning. Is everything alright?"

At that, Aud burst into tears and ran to her room.

Mai looked at Jake with bewilderment.

"I'm sorry, what did I say?"

Jake gestured for her to sit next to him and when she did, he grasped her hands in his, looking at her soberly.

"There's been a kidnapping during the night. Actually, more than one person. From what my dad has been able to find out from the town constable, it appears that six children from town are missing, including Aud's best friend."

"No!" Mai gasped. "What happened? Do they know where they were taken?"

Jake shook his head. "Not yet, but there's been some talk in town."

Jake looked at his dad in the kitchen who nodded, almost imperceptibly, then turned back to Mai. "Some of the town elders think the disappearances may be the work of a creature. Maybe even a troll, although it's been years since the last time this has happened."

Mai held up hand. "Wait. You're telling me that trolls are real as well?"

Mai sighed with dismay. As much as she quite enjoyed having more than just the usual human gifts, she didn't enjoy discovering the scary creatures considered to be evil in folklore also existed. She remembered Cat always complaining about this and couldn't help but agree with her now.

"So what happens now? If it is a troll, how do they operate? Do they have magic powers or something? How do we get the kids back?"

Mai couldn't believe she was asking the question, but it felt like they should be doing something. After all, if they had powers, it was up to them to keep the balance steady and right this wrong. Her friends weren't here to do it for her this time, so she knew she needed to step up and use her power to help.

"Traditionally, trolls like to live away from humans, in the mountains. Some legends say that Thor got rid of them all with lightning strikes, but others say that it's the town's church bells which keep them at bay. Unfortunately, and likely not coincidentally, the church's bells were recently taken down to be repaired. They were almost ready to be replaced and now this has happened." Anders answered Mai's question from where he was standing with Astrid and she turned to face him.

"Is this something that's happened before?" asked Mai, curious regarding why he seemed so certain of the cause.

Anders nodded. "The last time this happened was in the late eighteen hundreds, just before we built the current church. That's actually the reason it was constructed in the first place. Several children were kidnapped over a period of a few years and people were becoming afraid to leave their houses at night. The problem with trolls, though, is that they do have *some* magic. They can easily travel unseen by night. By the time morning comes, they've already disappeared, along with the victims they've stolen right from their beds."

In a small, tentative voice, Mai asked, "What do they do with them?"

Anders shrugged, but looked sad. "No one's sure, but they're never seen again. It's thought that they eat them, or maybe they can somehow turn them into another troll. But it's all speculation. We have nothing to go on, other than stories that have been passed down, but none that speak of victims who have ever escaped from such a fate."

"Jake, can we get them? What if we tried to follow the trail? Could we get there before they hurt them? Is that possible?"

Mai looked up at Jake, her eyes wide with concern and he smiled, cupping her cheek affectionately.

"We could, but it will likely be dangerous and uncomfortable. And it may mean a fight that we can't walk away from. Trolls are known to be quite violent."

Mai looked at the spot where Aud had been sitting before she'd raced off in tears and felt her resolve harden at the memory of her soon-to-be sister's devastation.

"I'd do it for any of *my* friends. Aud's best friend is missing, Jake. I can't let that be something that I don't at least try to fix."

Jake kissed her lightly on the nose with a look of mixed pride and gratitude, before standing up and going over to where his parents stood.

"Dad, how can we get as much information as possible? Surely, someone must have an idea where a troll would be living. It's not like the world is as big and hidden as it was a hundred years ago."

Anders clapped Jake on the shoulder, a pleased expression flitting over his face before he became somber once more.

"Of course, son. Let's go speak with my friends. I'm sure that one of them can fill you in. Mai, you're welcome to come with us as well, but your time may be better spent being fit for your dress this morning, if you're going to be away for awhile. As much as I hate to admit it, it's still an old boys club where I go for help. They'll probably be more open to questions if you aren't present. Astrid? What do you think?"

Astrid sighed and rubbed her forehead, arms crossed in front of her chest protectively. "Yes, that makes the most sense, I guess. We're needed here to protect the townsfolk, but Jake and his fiancée would be capable of going on this type of mission in our stead. Mai, I agree with Anders. Partially because of the residual sexism, but also because I would like the dress started."

Astrid temporarily looked irritated at the thought of the men, Mai assumed, but then continued with the same sad expression. "I also think your involvement will be limited because they'll most likely be more comfortable speaking in Norwegian, which means you may not understand them anyway."

Mai agreed without hesitation. She wasn't fond of strangers, so not going was fine with her. If Jake and his dad could get more information if she wasn't there, she might as well get the dress bit done, even if it niggled at her own burgeoning sense of equality of the sexes.

Only thirty minutes later, she waved goodbye to Jake and Anders, who left at the same time as they did for the men's meeting. She found herself taking a deep figurative breath as she waded into the feminine fray with her almost-mother-in-law.

Astrid was understandably subdued, but still seemed excited about getting Mai ready for the wedding, and was doing her best to smile and be friendly, which Mai appreciated.

"This shouldn't take too long, depending on the style of dress that you want. We can talk to the seamstress, get your measurements done, then swing by the flower shop next to look at what you'd like for the ceremony and reception, and then we'll speak with the caterer last. I'm hoping that we can be done everything by the time the men return, if that sounds okay with you? It's a big job, but then everything will be set for the date and ready when you return from searching."

Mai nodded, not quite sure it would be possible, but game to try. "Sure. I know exactly what I want so it shouldn't take long."

And it didn't. Mai had a very simple, traditional Chinese long gown in mind. When she explained it to the dressmaker Astrid had introduced her to, who thankfully spoke English, she'd merely nodded, then whipped out a tape measure, taking what felt like thirty different measurements before nodding again and shooing Mai and Astrid back out in under twenty minutes.

Astrid checked a box on her paper then nodded with satisfaction while Mai's head was still spinning from the rapidity of her dress fitting.

"The flower shop is just next door. He doesn't speak any English though, so just take a look and tell me what you're interested in, then I'll handle the rest."

Mai walked into a lush jungle of a shop, with hanging plants and flowers covering every free surface that wasn't decorated with picture books of floral arrangements. She stopped to flip through the pages of one of the books and called Astrid over, pointing out the flowers she held a special fondness for.

"This one's my favorite. They're the flower for the city of San Francisco. It would be nice to have something familiar at the wedding."

Astrid looked at the page and nodded. "I'll check on costs and availability."

She walked over to speak with the man behind the counter, returning shortly with a satisfied expression.

"He assures me that he'll be able to procure the necessary flowers for the wedding at a reasonable cost. We're done here. Let's speak with the caterer next. She's very busy but because she's a close friend of mine, she's promised to squeeze us in. I'm sure she'll make us coffee and kaffe kake. After all, she must advertise her goods."

Astrid surprised Mai by giving her a wink as they left the shop. They walked a short distance to a nearby house where Astrid knocked on the door.

"Hilde, det er Astrid her. Er du hjemme?"

They waited a few minutes until finally, Mai heard the sound of footsteps getting closer.

"Kommer! Jeg kommer!"

A small woman with messy brown hair answered the door, appearing slightly out of breath. When she saw who was there, she stood up erect and smiled, switching effortlessly into english.

"Oh, goodness, come in. I didn't expect you so soon! I was just tidying in the kitchen. You must be Mai; it's so nice to meet you!"

She stepped back from the door and gestured for them to enter. Astrid led the way while Mai looked curiously around the comfortable building. It wasn't as big as Jake's childhood home, but nonetheless it seemed cozy, with crocheted doilies on the back of the couches and a fantastic smell in the air. The woman had obviously been baking. Mai looked at her suspiciously when she saw a little twinkle in the woman's eyes, but didn't say anything until Astrid noticed her suspicious gaze and laughed with delight.

"Yes, Mai, she also has secrets she keeps from the regular human world. Part of why she's such a gifted baker, really. We have different names for them, but she's much like your Mr. Brown from Scotland whom Jake has told me about. She's our local version of a brownie."

Mai nodded, hardly surprised. It seemed like otherworldly things were more common in this town than what she'd experienced in the States. Maybe it was the small town itself, or maybe it was because the locals had grown up believing in their fairy tales, she couldn't be sure.

Hilde ended up making the most delicious cake that Mai had ever tasted. After her first taste of the indulgent treat, she was more than happy to let the other two women plan the menu. Astrid had already divulged that Anders and herself would be paying for the wedding earlier, so Mai didn't feel as attached to decisions about the food. She knew that her friends would eat anything as long as it was delicious. And after trying the cake, Mai was confident that anything Hilde made for them to eat would be amazing. Mai spent most of the time listening to the two women throw ideas around in a mix of English and Norwegian, while she nodded with a mouth full of one sample or another. It was so much easier than trying to interrupt and it allowed her mind to wander back to Jake. She wondered if he'd discovered anything about the troll and the missing children. By the time ten thirty rolled around, the two women were satisfied with the menu, and Mai was stuffed.

Mai gratefully said goodbye to the caterer. They walked the few blocks back to the house, all the boxes on Astrid's list checked off and a pleased Astrid to show for their efforts. However, Mai had already put the plans to the back of her mind, eager to hear what the men had discovered.

JAKE FELT OUT OF PLACE, yet strangely at home as he entered the diner with his father. Just as he remembered from his childhood, men sat around in varying styles of work attire, drinking coffee and discussing the day. Usually, the discussions were about what the fishing was like or about politics and news, but today the diner had a darker air. Jake stayed behind his father, silently watching as a man he recognized as the minister clapped his father on the back and shook his head.

While he'd only spoken Norwegian with his family over the last few years, Jake was grateful to find that he was able to keep up with the conversation easily.

"Anders. I'm glad to see you here. We welcome your presence and any help that you may be able to give us."

Anders gripped the hand on his shoulder and gave it a quick squeeze.

"Of course. My family and I will always be here to protect the village, whenever possible. What do you know?"

Jake listened silently as the minister spoke, watching as other men came and formed a loose grouping around them. The men stood with set jaws, none of them speaking, but the anger and grief on their faces obvious in their silence. Jake felt helpless with his own rage. He knew some of the kids that had gone missing, particularly Aud's friend, who'd been at his house so many times throughout the years she almost felt like another sister.

"I had a dream."

A man approached from the back of the group. Without a word, the men parted to let him move closer to Jake and his father. The man was old and frail, with a long white beard and a weather-beaten fisherman's cap on his head. He tottered forward, using a cane for support, and Jake leapt forward to steady him. The man smiled and squinted, looking carefully at his face.

"Ah, Jake Larsen. Just who I was looking for. You were there, as well as a girl with long dark hair. You must go to them, quickly. Follow the path of the troll along the river and be careful you do not lose yourself on the way."

Jake drew back in surprise, feeling a pit form in his stomach. The man's eyes were blurry and seemed to have cataracts, but somehow Jake knew that this man could see further than he could with his clear eyes. The man bobbed his head several times, then muttered under his breath before he tottered away the other direction, the men again parting to let him pass by.

"I see Jorgen is still alive. I haven't seen him in months and was wondering. This is good." Anders nodded as though he'd just received a pleasant surprise.

The minister leaned toward Anders. "Ja. He's getting older and more reclusive, maybe a little crazy in his old age, but his dreams are still sound."

The minister then turned to Jake. "You must do as he says, and follow the path. We believe that they have been taken to Hardangervidda. We don't know how long you have, but if Jorgen had a dream, we at least have hope that it's possible for you to succeed."

Jake felt his shoulders stiffen and he nodded his head once. He would bring the children home, if it was the last thing he did.

MAI WAS HAPPY TO SEE that Jake and Anders had beaten them back to the house. Yet when she opened the door, she was surprised to find that Jake had already packed their backpacks, almost running right into them as she stepped into the house. She could see that he'd filled them lighter than when they'd brought them across the ocean, but she was sure they were still full of the necessary equipment for hiking and camping. When

Mai looked up, she saw Jake and his dad sitting at the kitchen table, talking quietly to each other.

When Jake saw them enter, he jumped up.

"What did you find out?" Mai asked, rushing to speak first, both curious and afraid.

"It was as Dad feared. There's been talk of the trolls. The men think they're hiding in Hardangervidda National Park. It has a large expanse of rocky land and is sparsely populated. It's also known as a place where hikers have gone missing over the years. It seems to be as good a place to start as any, especially with the history of strange disappearances there."

Jake took a breath before he spoke quietly again. "One of Dad's friends says he had a dream, telling him that we should look there."

Mai squeezed his shoulder, no longer disbelieving when people said things like that. His words triggered a memory of her dream from the night before and she wondered if she'd heard or seen something herself, whether the noise she'd heard had been in the dream, or if somehow she'd heard one of the children as they'd been taken.

"I thought I heard a child crying last night in my dreams, but I completely forgot about it until just now. But I think maybe it means they're still alive? At least, they were when they were taken." Mai shook her head at the awful alternative and continued. "Are we ready to leave? I don't want to waste any time if it could mean the difference between life or death."

Jake rubbed the back of his neck then nodded.

"Bags are packed and ready. You just need to change into your hiking clothes and bring your cell phone, although we likely won't have any reception where we're going."

Mai inclined her head in acknowledgement and quickly went to change. When she returned, she saw that Astrid had packed a small bag of food, which Jake tucked into the top of his back pack before putting it on and holding Mai's bag up to help her. She strapped it on, giving his parents a small smile.

"Thanks for your hospitality. I hope to see you both soon."

Anders gave her a smile, but Astrid surprised her with a quick hug.

"Be careful out there. Keep your eyes open. There are many creatures out there that are hungry for human company. Watch over my son, please. Many of the dark creatures have no hesitation in keeping handsome young men."

Astrid looked at Mai fiercely and Mai felt she was trying to give her a message, although she wasn't sure about what.

Mai agreed instead of trying to decipher the cryptic warning. "Of course. I'll protect him with my last breath."

Astrid sighed and stepped back before hugging Jake. "You too, Jake. Protect her. I'd like to have strong dragon grandchildren, someday soon."

Jake hugged her back, giving her a kiss on the top of her head. "Yes, Mom. I will. Don't worry, we'll call if we can."

With those words spoken, Jake turned and opened the door, letting Mai exit first into the bright day.

CHAPTER TEN

The road became rocky immediately after leaving town. The landscape was harshly beautiful and Mai watched the barren lands and the sky above with wonder, unaccustomed to such large expanses of earth. Living in the city her entire life, she was used to many things being crammed into a single city block. But out here, the sky seemed to come alive with a blue background and the splash of clouds that scuttled above them. Given the breathing land and a sky that seemed to possess a magic of its own, Mai could understand why it seemed that so many Norwegians still knew the old stories and ways, and why they'd immediately thought of a troll as the reason for kidnapping, instead of a creepy human.

In San Francisco, or even in the towns where Cat and Vanessa had lived, if children had gone missing it would have immediately been assumed that a thirty-something, white male serial killer was behind the disappearance, or worse, that a close relative or acquaintance had been responsible. Mai found herself strangely happy to think that it wasn't people being awful for a change. It made the reality of missing children easier for her to cope with if it was an evil creature, instead of the everyday evil that lived in ordinary humans.

They'd walked for a few hours by the time Jake pulled them over to an outcropping of rocks near a small stream.

"Let's take a break to have some food and water," he said. "We can refill our bottles here before we continue."

"Sure. I was starting to get thirsty anyway. How far is it to the area where the men think the trolls are?" She passed her bottle to Jake to fill.

He squinted at the sun before looking over to the stream, then handed back her bottle.

"At least a solid day's travel. It kind of depends, but there isn't a faster way unless we want to go as dragons. But even that only helps if we travel by water. I don't find I have any more stamina hiking that way, plus, it kind of feels weird. There isn't much water between here and there and I think it's better to be seen as two average human hikers. If we get captured or spotted by a troll, we want to be seen as nonthreatening and weak."

"Makes sense," said Mai, as she took a sip from the bottle, adding, "I just hope that we aren't too late."

Jake twisted his mouth with worry. "Me too, Mai, me too. I know most of those kids. Heck, I babysat some of them. It hurts to think of what they may be going through. But we'll get them before it's too late, I'm sure of it."

Jake stood up and stretched. He looked around and pointed out another group of rocks beside the river a bit further away.

"I'm going to go use the facilities, okay? Holler if you need anything."

Mai nodded and turned the other way to give him privacy. She looked off into the sky, watching a few birds fly lazily by and occupied herself with the barren beauty around her, until she gradually realized it was a little too quiet when the birds suddenly flew away.

She turned to look over to where she'd seen Jake go and realized that she couldn't hear or see him any longer. Curious and more than a little worried, she stood up then hesitated. Maybe he'd just bent down, or was, um, squatting or something, she thought, still not wanting to interrupt anything. But after waiting a few seconds longer, she sighed, and began to walk toward the direction where she'd last seen him.

No Jake. The other side of the rocks was empty, except for his water bottle. It was tipped over onto one side, with a small puddle of water underneath it and had almost stopped dripping. Mai looked toward the river and saw not even a ripple on the surface. The water had become curiously calm, almost resembling a lake of glass. Mai could feel the wrongness of the water and knew that she wasn't alone. She allowed her power to fill her then reached her mind into the stream, questing for what was disturbing her sense of the water and causing an eerie chill to ripple down her spine.

At first, she couldn't tell what was happening, but as she delved deeper, she saw a shadow of darkness and knew that another being of water, a dark creature, was hiding in the depths of a rocky crag close to where Jake had disappeared moments earlier. She allowed her body to ripple and change into her dragon form, feeling a low growl rumble through her chest.

Mai dove into the water, cutting through it with surgical precision and heading to the area of rocks she'd seen filled with the darkness. The colour of the river bottom changed from smooth, light-brown gravel at the edges, to a dark green mildewed slime, which became progressively fouler the closer she approached. She felt her mind assailed by the impurity there and found it hard to reconcile the surrounding darkness at the bottom with what had looked so innocent on the surface.

This was obviously the home of something evil. Mai approached cautiously, ready for a surprise attack from any direction. She silently glided up to the largest rock and peaked out from behind it. As she'd expected, something *was* lurking there. The creature's back was toward her and in front of it, she saw Jake.

His eyes were closed and he was in his human form, floating, but tied into place with a cord made of a greenish substance. She wasn't sure what the creature was, as it didn't resemble anything she'd ever seen before. It appeared vaguely human in shape, with long hair-like tendrils that extended down its back and a misshapen appearance, as though it had been squashed by something much larger.

As Mai watched, it seemed to shift shape, becoming longer and more serpentine as it adjusted the cord holding Jake down. It looked like it was readying itself to wrap it around his neck. The rage that Mai had been holding back bubbled up inside her. Anger at the thing that had taken her man, anger at the reason they were out here, anger at everything that she'd been holding down for so long.

The growl slipped out before she even knew that she was doing it and the creature whipped around to look right at her. Her view from the front wasn't any better. Now she could see that it had weird insect-like features and large eyes that glowed an ugly, eerie yellow. It appeared surprised to see a greenish-blue dragon behind a rock, but the monster's initial immobility quickly dissipated and it began to advance.

Mai knew her chance to observe was over. It was time to fight. She dove towards the creature before it had a chance to get any closer to her. Using her strong tail, she caught the creature around its midsection and squeezed as hard as she could while she roared with rage. Her anger overwhelmed her, swelling up until she felt her vision blur into whiteness and then fade completely.

When she opened her eyes, she was horrified. There in her grip was a broken, unmoving body. She dropped it and moved back in stunned disbelief. She hadn't even been threatened before she'd acted. It may have meant her no harm, but her anger at seeing Jake imprisoned had overwhelmed her usual conciliatory nature and caused her to attack first. She gasped in the water at her actions before gliding toward Jake, still in shock at what she'd done.

Jake remained unmoving, oblivious to what had transpired. He seemed to be in a trance of some kind, but Mai was relieved to see his chest was still rising and falling. Thankful they could both breathe underwater, she quickly snapped the cord holding him. She carried him gently, gripping his smaller human frame in her claws as she rose to the surface with her precious cargo.

Looking around as she surfaced, Mai realized that they'd been in a small pond just off the main river that was enclosed by trees and rocks. She dragged Jake's limp body out of the water and shifted back into her human form to better assess him. She bent over him to listen for signs of breathing, relieved when she heard air moving easily back and forth from his mouth. Looking around for landmarks, she observed their bags on the other side of the river and sighed. She needed dry clothes and Jake needed help. Debating whether or not to get their stuff and come back, or take Jake back to the other side, she decided to take him with her. She didn't want him out of her sight until she knew what had happened and whether or not there were any other threats close by.

Quickly, she relocated them and changed her clothing, looking around warily all the while. She had no idea what to do now. He was still unconscious, or under a spell, and she didn't know how to snap him out of it. Worry rattled her nerves. What if she hadn't killed that creature? What if there were more of them? She didn't even know what that monster had been. She was so far out of her comfort zone at the moment that she felt paralyzed by her lack of knowledge. The hot sting of tears pricked her eyes but she swiped at them angrily. She didn't have time to indulge, not now.

Jake coughed, then moaned slightly. Mai turned back to him with hope, her heart rising when she saw his eyes flutter open. She knelt down close to his face again.

"Jake, are you okay? What happened? What was that thing?"

Mai touched his cold cheek worriedly and he weakly grabbed at her hand, squeezing it lightly before giving her a half-smile. She'd never been so happy to see such a pitiful smile before and Mai felt the tight knot of worry loosen in her chest.

"Hey, babe. That was something, hey?"

Mai waited for an explanation, but he just laid his head back down on the ground and closed his eyes. Frustrated, Mai looked around, checking the perimeter again to make sure nothing was sneaking up on them before she gently shook his shoulder.

"Jake, wake up. It's important. Are we safe? Is there more of those...things?"

Jake opened his eyes again, looking a little more awake this time, and struggled to sit up.

"Sorry, I'm just so tired right now." He punctuated his reply with a yawn. "I'm pretty sure we just met a nyk. I don't know very much about them, but from what I remember, I'm pretty sure they like to work solo."

Jake managed to sit up and Mai was glad to see that he seemed to be more awake now. He'd propped his body up, using his elbows to support his weight on his knees. Mai handed him some water which he accepted gratefully, guzzling it down, then wiping his mouth off.

"I don't know what happened. One minute I was just about done, you know," Jake replied, blushing. "I was coming back to see if you were ready to leave, then the next minute, I kind of went foggy and it was like I was in a dream under water. I remember feeling calm, almost as if I was floating. I think I saw you under there too, but that's it, except for the face."

Jake paused to shudder at the memory.

"I remember hearing about the nyk, sometimes called nokken, back when I was a kid. I'd always thought that it was just a story to keep us out of strange lakes and stuff, something our parents told us to keep us nearby when we were out swimming." Jake laughed dryly. "But I guess not."

He stopped talking to look at her curiously. "How did you get me away from it? They have the ability to hypnotize people, which I'm guessing is what they did to me."

Mai's cheeks slowly darkened and she looked away in shame.

"I lost my temper. I've brought dishonour to myself. I grabbed the creature in rage even before it attacked me and I squeezed it as hard as I could. I felt something in it crack. I was so surprised and horrified at my loss of control that I left it on the floor of the pond and took you away, bringing you up to the surface."

Mai looked up, feeling that same prick of tears but not wanting to allow them to fall and compound her shame.

"I don't know if it's alive or dead. I just couldn't bear that it had taken you away from me. I feel awful. I'm not sure if you can forgive me, or look at me the same way now. I'm a murderer."

Mai continued to look at her hands, feeling sorrow for her actions. She didn't know this creature. She'd acted on emotion against something that looked frightening and had taken a loved one. That wasn't the kind of person she was and she was ashamed of her instinctive reaction. What if it hadn't really been evil? Even when she'd been fighting Dub and the other soulless creatures that had been evil, she'd never felt this loss of control, had never killed from a place of anger. She felt sick.

Jake reached over and pulled her into his arms, causing them to both topple over onto the ground. He wasn't strong enough to hold her up yet, but he cradled her in his arms as they lay there, looking her straight in the eye as he spoke.

"Mai, you were amazing. You saved my life. The nyk doesn't let go of its victims, and in the stories I've heard, most are never seen again. I don't know if you killed it or not, but it was most definitely evil and you have absolutely nothing to apologize for. I'm not sure if I feel strong enough to keep walking yet, but I want to move a little further away from the water right now. I know I said they usually work alone, but I don't want to chance it."

Jake struggled to sit up after giving her another hug, so Mai helped him to stand once they'd managed to achieve a sitting position. He swayed a little, and looked paler than usual, but after a few moments she saw him become steadier and his color improve.

"I think I'm okay now, as long as we walk slowly."

Mai looked doubtfully up at him and he scowled at her.

"I'm fine," he insisted.

Mai shrugged and picked up her bag.

"Are you good enough to carry your bag, or do you want me to do that for awhile?"

Jake took his bag a little churlishly from her, but after a few seconds, she saw his shoulders relax and he shot her a rueful grin.

"Sorry. Apparently, having my manliness questioned makes me cranky. I'm feeling better now, really. Let's just take it easy for a bit. Hopefully we can make it to the caves before nightfall."

They walked slower than normal for the first hour as they picked their way further from the river they'd been following. Neither was completely certain that Mai had actually killed the nyk and they didn't want to stay close enough to find out. This meant that the landscape became even more rocky as they ranged further from the river and the terrain became more difficult and hilly. At one point, they were walking up and down large hills that reminded Mai of the areas they'd hiked in back home, with the main exception being far fewer trees.

As the sky began to darken, they came to the area of caves that Jake had wanted to reach by nightfall. He'd regained his energy throughout the day and Mai relaxed as he returned to his usual self. They'd decided that he'd most likely been under a spell of some sort and that it had faded with time and distance away from the nyk.

Mai hadn't liked how weak and dazed he'd been, even more than she hadn't liked her violent reaction to something that had scared her. Hopefully, neither event would happen again. But if she was honest with herself, she knew that she'd always go on the defensive if she felt a loved one was in danger, no matter what the fallout. She wasn't sure how she felt about that new understanding, but it changed her feelings about her identity, knowing she had that side to herself.

Jake approached the entrance of a small, darkened depression in the rock wall, looking in cautiously. Mai could see his shoulders sink back to their normal relaxed position and knew that he'd found a safe harbour for them.

He confirmed her thought almost immediately.

"Let's stay here tonight. From what the men in the village said, I think the place where the trolls are supposed to be is only a few hours away. This is a small cave, with no other opening except this one, so we know there isn't anything lurking in here. We should be safe to rest here for a few hours then move on when the sun comes back at dawn. Trolls don't like being out in the day, so we'll stand a better chance at catching them by surprise and beating them if we wait until we have an advantage."

Mai nodded, but hesitated. "What about the kids? Shouldn't we keep moving?"

Jake's brown furrowed. "Maybe, but it's not a good idea to keep moving out here with darkness falling. Even if we don't come upon anything that wants to kill and eat us, the land itself is dangerous. We could easily get hurt or fall into a crevice and be trapped. It's better to wait until dawn and hope that nothing happens to them until then. We've got to be able to get them back to town and that means keeping ourselves safe too."

Mai sighed, knowing he was right.

"Okay. Should we make a fire or something?"

Jake shook his head. "No. It would draw attention. Plus, it's too small inside. It would get too smoky in here and possibly even give us carbon monoxide poisoning. We can sleep in dragon form for comfort, warmth, and to discourage any interest from anyone or anything that may be passing in the night." Jake smiled. "Even a troll would think twice about bothering a sleeping dragon."

Mai snorted. Jake in human form wasn't the easiest to wake up in the morning some days, and in dragon form, he could literally bite someone's head off if he got angry.

"Sure, that sounds good."

Mai put her backpack against the back wall of the cave and let the familiar tingling in her body erupt, turning into the long serpentine form that felt so natural now. She cautiously turned her larger form around in a large circle, assessing the cave for any large rocks before she settled into a curled up ball like a large, scaly kitten. Jake followed suit, putting his stuff along the opposite wall and changing into his dragon form and curling around her. They nuzzled for a few moments, enjoying the shared warmth of their bodies before closing their eyes and falling into exhausted slumber.

CHAPTER
ELEVEN

Morning dawned with crisp air carrying the day over the rocks. Mai woke to gentle light falling into the cave, highlighting the grey walls and floor of their overnight lodgings. She looked beside her and felt her heart slow with contentment when she saw Jake, still sleeping. As always, she loved watching him, but today she was just happy to see him there, after the events of the day before.

Nudging his jaw with her snout, she pushed against him. He growled lightly in his sleep until she nipped him, then licked his small injury better. His golden, slit-like pupil became visible under a half-open lid and she saw his eye dilate with the light. He rolled onto his back, leaving his belly exposed for her and she took advantage of the weakness, nipping along his neck playfully. He let out a louder growl before he rolled, putting her underneath his larger body and nipping her back.

She smiled with childlike glee. "Good morning, my love."

Even in dragon form, he was the most attractive individual she'd ever met and she could feel her temperature climbing. Remembering that they were on a mission, and thinking of the missing children cooled her down, and her smile faded.

Jake noticed and nuzzled her nose gently with his own.

"Good morning, love."

He spoke gently before turning his back, transforming back into the sturdy golden man she'd first fallen in love with. She watched his firm backside longingly for a second before shaking her head and standing up, feeling her own skin tingle and shift as she changed. Pulling on her clothes from the previous day, with the addition of clean socks and underwear, Mai dressed quickly and was ready at the same time as Jake.

They ate the plain food Jake had packed the day before, which was more than enough to fill their empty stomachs for the day's walk, then repacked their supplies. Jake pulled out his map, showing Mai a drawing one of the town elders had made. It appeared that they merely had to cross the next range of low mountains beside the sea before they reached their goal. Mai knew it couldn't be as easy as the drawing implied. Once she looked out the entry of the cave, she groaned. The sky was grey and it looked like rain would be their companion for the day, which was sure to increase the difficulty of the hike.

They checked the map one more time, then headed north to the sea as soon as they had finished packing up. The weather quickly became wilder as the wind picked up strength. Mai began to have trouble seeing as the wind whipped up dust from the rocky ground, needing to squeeze her eyes shut multiple times to avoid the grit that was flying through the air. As they drew closer to the sea, the sky turned black and whitecaps were visible as far as they could see. A fierce howling rose above the sound of the crashing waves and Mai turned a wide-eyed gaze to Jake.

He scanned the surface of the water.

"I don't know what that sound is. It sounds like someone screaming," he said, sounding concerned.

Suddenly, a glowing shape appeared on the water, rowing what looked like a small boat with two oars. The tall, gaunt figure had the shape of a hooded man, and Mai had the sensation of ice rise up along the back of her neck, as she recalled the dreadful image of a prior foe. The figure looked like Dub, the dark soul-stealer that she'd first met when he'd turned her into stone over a hundred years earlier, and Mai took an involuntary step back from the water. Jake placed a calming hand on her back.

Mai shook her head repeatedly. "No. It's not possible. It can't be. Cat killed him, we saw it happen!"

Mai wasn't comforted by Jake's touch for the first time she could remember, but he still tried to rub her shoulder reassuringly, even as she pulled away.

"Shh, shhhh min livs kjærlighet. It's not him. I know of this one. He's native to these parts. He's dangerous, but not unbeatable."

Mai looked at him, curiosity replacing some of her fear, and waited for him to continue.

Jake cleared his throat. "I've only heard about them in passing, but I believe it's a draugr. It's still very dangerous, but we're safe right now, since we aren't actually on the water."

"What do you mean?" Mai asked, doubtful that it was completely safe, given the unearthly appearance of the creature in the rowboat.

"I mean it generally attacks sailors, which we aren't. And even if we were on the water, we can both breathe under it, so the creature can't drown us the way it usually does with its victims."

Jake paused, wrinkling his nose in thought.

"I'm actually not sure why it likes to drown people. I never heard that part of the story. Basically, it's another old wive's tale I used to hear as a kid that I thought was just to get us to come back to the house if it started raining and became stormy. You know, 'the draugr'll get you if you don't come in out of the rain,' that kind of thing."

Jake mimed his mom scolding him and Mai's lips quirked, some of her fear fading with her amusement of the image of a small Jake racing into the house to avoid a monster. She'd always been scared of being hit by lightning, so a bogeyman wouldn't have been needed to get her to go inside.

"So you think we're fine to stay here?" Mai asked, her voice lifting in hope.

"Should be, but let's not take any chances. We should keep moving. I really don't want to have to try to beat a water demon with our water powers. I don't think we'd have much of an advantage."

Nodding, Mai sped up her steps and they quickly moved further away from the water and closer to the mountains.

Unfortunately, Jake had been wrong when he'd thought the draugr only went for sailors. Even though they'd sped up, the rowboat continued to advance on them. Mai looked back over her shoulder a few minutes after they'd started to move inland. With mounting fear, she saw that he was now close enough for her to make out his features. The draugr appeared human, but with skin so grey in colour and so wrinkled that she imagined it was what a man who'd been underwater for several weeks would look like. His hair was stringy and matted against his face and his eyes were hollowed out holes. Mai thought she could see a skull looking back at her, but turned away before she could get a closer look. Her stomach wasn't up for the challenge.

"Jake, look!" she hissed, yanking on his arm as he continued to walk, not looking back. "It's getting closer and I think it sees us. It looks like it's coming right for us now. What do we do?"

Jake reluctantly turned his head to look, obviously feeling the same way Mai did when it came to examining the face of underwater death.

"I don't know. I never heard what one does to avoid a draugr, except staying inside during storms."

Mai shook her head with exasperation. He wasn't being very helpful, so she quickly scanned their surroundings. They were getting closer to the mountains, but were still on a long, rocky beach too close to the draugr, who seemed to be gaining on them. There wasn't any cover to hide behind, barring the mountains, and it was moving much faster than they were, so it wasn't looking good for their chances at getting to a hiding place within the mountains first. That meant that they'd have to fight if it came after them, Mai realized with dread.

While she'd used her powers to fight soul-suckers in the past, Mai knew she wasn't the strongest fighter. She'd usually been heavily supported by Cat's fire magic or Vanessa's hurricane-force gales. She could drown a victim, use water to surround them, or even use her dragon strength, and had even accidentally eaten someone once, but that didn't seem to be enough to deal with another creature comfortable with her water element.

She searched her mind, not coming up with any ideas until she looked at Jake and remembered when they'd fought Dub on the bridge as dragons. Not only were they physically stronger in that form, but she thought that her magic was more focused as well.

"Jake, I know you didn't want to show up in dragon shape when we were close to the trolls, but I think that's our best chance at getting away from the draugr. Unless you have a better idea?"

Mai raised an eyebrow, hoping that Jake had something miraculous to throw out that would save them. Instead, he agreed.

"Yeah, I wanted to surprise the trolls and have them think that we were just hikers, but I've got nothing else for ideas. So, dragons it is. Let's leave our stuff over here behind this rock."

Jake pointed to a small outcropping where he deposited his bag and Mai added her bag to his.

"It's as good a place as any. You ready?"

Even as she spoke, Mai quickly shed her clothes and allowed the familiar and welcoming tingle to spread quickly through her body. She stretched into her full, almost ten-foot length, of her favourite self. She always felt vibrantly alive as a dragon. If it wasn't so isolating from other people, she'd often thought she could live happily ever after in her lovely azure shape. She smiled as she looked over her shoulder to see her handsome, golden, soon-to-be husband shining under the rain that was falling onto his scales.

"I'm ready. How do you want to do this?" he asked, tilting his large head to the side in question.

Mai shook her head, knocking the rain off her face with mild irritation at the tickling sensation.

"Let's get closer to the water. I don't want our packs getting trashed in a fight if we can avoid it. I think we should be ready to try to trap him with water, but I also think it may come down to physically overpowering him, if necessary."

Jake nodded and they walked together towards the beach, stopping a few feet away from the surf that pounded white froth onto the rocks. Mai felt her heart in her throat as the glowing inhuman creature came closer. As they waited, it rowed onto the shore. But instead of getting out and coming towards them, it waited, silently watching them. Mai began to feel uncomfortable. Why wasn't he approaching? What was he waiting for? She looked at Jake in confusion, but only received a small, uncertain shrug in response. Looking back at the creature, she was again repulsed by its hollowed out eyes and seaweed crusted hair.

Finally, the creature spoke. Its voice was like a death shriek, causing Mai to feel as though ice was dripping down her scales.

"What do you do here? This is my territory. Dragons are not welcome here!"

Mai listened to the words and felt her confusion grow. Not only was it speaking in a way that she could understand, but it seemed more ticked off at them than deadly. She looked at Jake with stunned amusement and suspected that he was having similar thoughts.

"What do you mean, your territory?"

Jake spoke as calmly as he could, but Mai heard a telltale squeak as his voice cracked slightly on the word 'your'. He sounded and looked tough otherwise, which impressed Mai.

Turning her attention back to the draugr, she winced as she observed its now petulant and ugly face.

It answered Jake's question truculently. If Mai wasn't mistaken, it almost looked s though it was pouting. "These are my hunting grounds. You are not welcome to have the sailors and hikers that get lost here. What did you do with the pair that I just saw? They looked delicious. I was looking forward to drowning them and eating their life force."

Mai felt her temper start to simmer and was ready to answer until Jake cut her off.

"You're too late. They were indeed delicious. We've been travelling a long time and were hungry. I do apologize. We had no idea that this area was already claimed. We shall continue on our way and leave any other takings for your enjoyment."

Mai choked back a giggle. Jake trying to sound heartless and blasé about murder rang false to her and she'd never tell him, but she didn't think he was a very good actor, even though he'd been doing it for years. His face was too honest and kind in her opinion to ever pull off a bad guy role. But apparently, his lie worked, because the draugr shook his fist angrily at them before turning the row boat around and yelling at them from over his shoulder.

"If you were not already leaving I'd be tempted to take you on myself. But as long as you leave now, this is over. If I see you again however, I will make you pay."

Letting out another ungodly shriek, the draugr quickly rowed away and within a few minutes, the glow from the creature had completely faded, leaving Jake and Mai alone on the beach in the rain.

Mai burst out laughing and Jake began to chuckle as well. First slowly, then hard enough that they fell to the ground, with laughter and relief overwhelming them both.

"You mean to tell me that a scary, man-eating, drowning-people creature is also a spoiled brat?" Mai asked, only able to get a few words out at a time between sobs of laughter.

Jake was by now laying flat on his back, chest moving up and down in laughter as well. "Seems so." He howled at the image. After a few minutes he was able to gasp out a few more words. "Well, at least we didn't have to fight with any more skill than a middle-school girl."

Mai felt tears come to her eyes. She was laughing so hard that she was crying and only sobered up when she felt her tears starting to turn into a river. She didn't want to add to the deluge falling around them, so she took a few deep breaths and tried to calm down. She hadn't cried a river since Vanessa, Cat, and Evelyn had found her in the form of a stone dragon in the park and it was a strong enough reminder that her good humor faded away, replaced by caution.

"We got lucky this time, Jake. But I think that this is a warning to get back under cover. It may still be daytime, but it's almost as dark as night right now with these thick clouds. We're sitting ducks, or dragons, in this case. We've been walking a long time and it's already into the afternoon. How much further do you think the troll caves are? Should we wait out the storm and try again in the morning?"

Jake looked for his watch and Mai could see the moment of frustration when he remembered that he didn't wear one in dragon form. Mai watched him shift back to human and her stomach tingled in anticipation as she looked at him.

While they hadn't gone all the way yet, they'd been naked around each other many times, in the way people comfortable in their own skin often could be. Mai had no insecurities about her own body as human or dragon, but felt herself flush every time Jake was exposed around her. Once again, the same low-down fire started in her belly, making her glance down and away from him. If he'd ever noticed her looking, he'd never said anything, and was always careful to give her space. She'd never once seen him looking at her naked body in return and some-times, she wondered if he wasn't attracted to her in the same way. He was always able to act so relaxed and nonchalant and had never been anything other than gentlemanly when they'd shifted.

She certainly didn't feel like that when he was naked around her. It was all she could do not to stare at his well-toned body. And the worst part about the whole thing for her was that it was completely her fault that they weren't already fully familiar with each other. Mai cursed her prudish ways, as she did each time she saw him like this, but forced herself to focus on the matter at hand.

Jake had found his watch as he got dressed, his back to her and seemingly oblivious to her turmoil, he answered her earlier question.

"It looks like we have a few more hours of daylight." He looked up at the clouds and sighed. "But I don't think it's actu-ally going to be sunny. It looks like we are going to have rain all day, based on those clouds."

Mai pursed her lips and looked at the sky.

"So what should we do then? Find a cave? Keep going?"

Jake nodded. "That's probably the best plan. If the day is this dark, trolls have no problem coming out into the light. All we can do is hope that the kids are safe until we get to them and that tomorrow is a sunnier day."

Mai agreed, but was becoming frustrated that the weather and the landscape itself seemed to be conspiring against them. They ate more of the packed food where they were before lucking out on a small indent between two rocks a short time later. It was hardly big enough for one person let alone two, but because it looked sheltered and safe, they decided to squeeze into the space in human shape and share body heat.

"Here, let me go in first. You can arrange yourself however is most comfortable once I'm settled."

Ever the gentleman, Jake offered to be her cushion and she gingerly settled herself down on his half-reclined position. He'd made a pillow out of his back pack and tucked hers in beside him, so it made a half-bed. Mai knew that he couldn't have been very comfortable, but he didn't complain as she tucked herself into his broad, warm chest. Mai felt herself melt into him. She didn't know how much longer she could bear this. She was alarmed by her thoughts, and becoming so impatient she knew that with even the slightest encouragement, they wouldn't be having a white wedding after all.

Jake caught her gaze with a flash of his golden eyes. She watched as they glowed with heat, making her breath catch in her suddenly dry throat. She felt the skin that touched hers heat up, her nerve endings tingling as they caught fire as well.

"Jake."

One word was all she was able to say before all other words dried up in her mouth and her eyes turned to water, still trapped in the golden warmth of his.

"Mai."

Jake groaned in what sounded like pain and Mai felt a thrill race through her. He wasn't immune after all.

"I can't be strong much longer. I'm really, really trying here."

Jake looked at her sincerely. In that moment, Mai knew that he was the most honorable person she'd ever met. And that was all it took. Something inside her broke off, flying away on the wind and rain. With all of the fear that had come from almost losing him earlier, as well as the fact that they were alone and far from civilization and judgment, her last vestige of willpower disappeared into the night. To her great surprise, she felt only relief at its passing.

Mai wrapped herself tighter around Jake and began roaming her hands over his muscled biceps and deltoids, having learned the names of the muscles in order to know what she'd been admiring on him from the day they'd first met. She felt goose bumps erupt, then smiled wickedly before nipping at his throat, hearing his breath catch before escaping raggedly.

He suddenly grabbed her, hands slipping down to hold her hips against him tightly. She felt molten lava pool lower, hotter, in her abdomen. She'd never known she could feel heat like this, never known that she had this much passion in her body. She'd always been reserved and held herself back, apart from those in the world around her. But with Jake, she wanted to be part of him, to curl up inside somewhere and stay with him forever.

Jake tilted her head towards his and she eagerly met his lips, feeling them searching, questing deep within her soul. This felt so right and Mai wasn't sure why she'd held back so long. As they kissed, frantic hands removed items of wet clothing, frustrated by the difficulty of the action. The jeans caused both of them to groan, then laugh, and they stopped part way through for more kisses.

Mai relished the feel of her bare chest against his rougher, hairy one and felt her heart rate sky rocket higher. As the last barriers between them fell away, Mai felt her breath completely leave her body. A high-pitched, keening sound left her mouth, quickly captured by Jake. They moved in the rain as one being and Mai felt her soul shatter into a million pieces before falling like shooting stars all around her.

Mai collapsed onto his chest as he shuddered. They lay still for a long time, holding tightly to each other in the night. The rain continued to fall around their cozy lair as they held on to love, falling asleep contentedly in each other's arms.

MAI SLEPT FOR WHAT felt like an eternity, tired and sore from the events of the day. She felt herself slowly rise back to consciousness as the light around her changed. When she opened her eyes, she saw Jake watching her, his smoldering, golden eyes half open, and smiled sleepily back at him.

"How do you feel?" he asked, his face filled with concern.

Mai smiled and gave him a kiss on the nose. "I feel silly."

He looked alarmed, then upset, so she quickly shook her head, smiling back even more to try to allay his fears.

"No, I don't regret a thing. I mean that I feel silly I made us wait this long. If I'd have known, if I'd realized..." Mai trailed off, still shaking her head. "I'll never know how you were so good to me. I think if our places had been reversed, I wouldn't have been able to wait."

Jake moved his hands to hold her face still and looked at her with as earnest a look as she'd ever seen.

"I'd crawl on my hands and knees to the end of the universe for you. I would *never* do anything that could cause you any distress or harm. You weren't ready, even though I could see you wanted to be. There's no way I would have or could have pushed that. It needed to be on your terms, you had to be the one to want me wholeheartedly or I'd just be some asshole guy, going after my own needs. I love you so much more than anything physical could ever show you."

She looked at him, at his honest, open expression, and promptly burst into tears.

"I didn't mean...I'm sorry! I'm so sorry!" Jake apologized, trying to get her to stop crying but she put her finger up to his lips, shushing him through her tears.

"Stop. It's not you. Everything that you've ever said or done for me has been perfect, Jake. You're more than I ever thought I'd have in my life and that's why I can't help myself. I'm crying because I have everything I've ever wanted, everything I never even knew I wanted, right here in you. I can only hope that I mean half as much to you as you do to me."

He relaxed against her, drawing her back into his arms for a full-body hug.

"Thank God. I was worried for a minute that I'd hurt you, or that you were regretting what just happened. This was the best moment of my life, narrowly beating the first time we met."

Mai smiled, wiped away her tears, then kissed him again.

"The night is young still. It looks like we have to wait a little bit before we can go looking for the children."

She bit her lip suggestively, raising an eyebrow as she drew back slightly, still naked. Mai watched as his eyes changed back to molten gold, then laughed throatily as he pulled her back down.

CHAPTER
TWELVE

M ai felt stiff in places she hadn't even known existed when she next awoke. She wasn't sure if it was from their nocturnal activities, or from sleeping in a tiny rock crevice half on top of Jake, but she was damn sore. She groaned as she rolled off Jake, feeling the cold wall against her back, and was startled by the shock of the temperature change. Of course, the space was so small she basically jumped back onto Jake, causing him to wake up as well.

He blinked his eyes open blearily until he saw her, naked and half-falling off him, then he smiled the lazy smile of a man who was thoroughly enjoying his view.

"Good morning." Jake continued to watch her lazily, hungrily, and Mai felt her cheeks turn red.

"I'm not sure what I'm supposed to act like today. I've never done this before." She looked at him nervously.

He smiled and he gave her a quick hug, warm and comforting, until he patted her butt, causing her to jump again.

Jake laughed. "You're amazing. It's us, Mai. You can act however you want. I love you and you love me. Now, while I'm totally open to having a long, leisurely cave experience for as long as you want, and I don't think boredom would set in for a long, *long* time, I also think that it's daylight and we have kids to save. Are you ready to get going?"

Mai pushed herself off Jake awkwardly and lifted her chin defensively. "Of course I am. I wouldn't put my wants before people that need us."

Jake groaned. "I'm sorry Mai, I didn't mean to have it come out like that. I just wanted you to know that I love you even more now and that I'd love to spend the next week discovering your body. But we both know we could never live with ourselves if we put that above people that need us."

Mai sighed, forcibly calming herself down. She was on edge and she knew it. He hadn't said anything offensive, and she knew he was trying to make her relax, but it wasn't working. Trying to put the incredible night behind them, Mai smiled brightly, if not completely honestly.

"I know what you meant, Jake, and it's okay. I'm just feeling strange, is all. Let's get dressed and find these kidnapping monsters as quickly as we can. I want to get home to our wedding as soon as humanly possible. You need to make an honest woman out of me now."

Jake watched her, finally nodding his head cautiously at her reply.

"Alright, as long as you're good. We should be really close, maybe within an hour away now. We'll need to be really quiet and try not to talk at all. But Mai, I want you to know that we can talk about this anytime you want, just not before we get there. Is that okay?"

Mai nodded. She knew that he felt as if he were walking on eggshells and she couldn't change that right now. It wasn't his fault that she was being all weird, well, not entirely. She'd made her choice and had been glad to get that milestone out of the way. But still, she felt a little like a fallen woman. Trying to get nineteenth century morality out of her head was harder than she could have imagined, even though she had no regrets otherwise.

"I get it. We don't want them to hear us coming. Do you think that we can get there today? Or will we need to wait through another night?"

Jake thought for a moment then shook his head.

"It's hard to say. It could go either way, depending on where the trolls are and where they're keeping the kids, not to mention what the weather decides to do today. From the tales I've heard, sometimes they keep their victims in kind of a cage, like a barn or something, and other times they separate them and keep them spread them out. It kind of depends on what they're planning to do with them."

Mai thought of the poor scared kids they were trying to find and her resolve hardened. "Well, we should get going now then. We haven't got any time to waste."

Once again, they ate quickly then packed, leaving their crevice behind. Mai glanced at it once over her shoulder as they walked away, knowing that she would always remember it fondly. It was the place where she felt that they'd truly joined, as if they'd already been married under the light of the stars in the rain; man and wife in the oldest way possible. The actual wedding ceremony was just a formality. She was already his forever.

———— ⬡ ————

JAKE HAD BEEN RIGHT, they were close. It was only about a half hour before they arrived at a sheer wall of rock that stretched into mountainous proportions. They both had a more powerful sense of smell than the average human, even when they weren't in dragon form, and Mai could see a dark depression about half way up from which the smell of fear seemed to be emanating. She looked at Jake, who had a fierce scowl on his face, nostrils flaring. She touched his arm and she could see him trying to breathe calmly, but she knew it was hopeless to even attempt to relax. These were children that Jake knew, including one that had likely been in his house many times as his little sister's friend. She couldn't imagine what he felt, but knew how upset she'd be if it was someone that she cared about who'd been taken. The way she'd felt when the Nyk had abducted Jake had been awful, even though it hadn't lasted long.

Jake turned to look at her, gesturing silently with his head over to the right side of the rock face. When she inspected it, she noticed a rough set of stairs hewn into the rock, hardly visible to the naked eye. That must have been how the children had been taken up there, she realized. She examined the wall for another entrance, but couldn't see anything obvious, which didn't bode well for a fast escape with small children.

Mai tugged on Jake's arm, attempting to make hand signals indicating they should look around for another entrance. Jake looked confused at first, then pointed to the entrances and held up two fingers, cocking his head as though asking a question, and she pointed.

Yes, was there another entrance?

He shrugged then made walking motions with his middle and pointer finger on his right hand, suggesting that they circle around.

Mai nodded. *Good idea*, she thought, gesturing for him to go first. He started walking again.

Careful not to make a sound on the loose rocks, they slowly picked their way around the face of the mountain, but it seemed to go on forever. They stopped and Jake shook his head. It looked as if this was their best choice to enter the cave. Mai once again felt her stomach sink. Nervous butterflies tried to crawl up her throat, but she pushed them back down.

It's not about you, silly, she scolded herself. *There are some frightened kids in there that are going to be a meal if you don't do something. You're a dragon, for goodness sake!*

She remembered the time she'd accidentally eaten someone and smiled. After all, it wasn't like she was completely helpless or anything. She felt her courage return and saw that Jake was waiting for her to follow him. She steeled her resolve and her expression hardened. Jake's eyes lit up with pride before he gestured for her to follow him.

The two dragons climbed up the mountain path, well disguised in their weak human hiker guise. Hoping against hope that they wouldn't encounter any trolls before they found the children, they kept their guard up and their eyes open. They waited at the mouth of the cave for a few minutes while their eyes adjusted to the dim light. During that brief moment, Mai could smell too many things. Fear, urine, and something that smelled as though it had been decaying for years.

She was alarmed at the thought that it could be one of the kids, but Jake grabbed her wrist insistently and made her look at him. He held his nose before doing a pantomime of a big lumbering giant and she choked back a nervous laugh, nodding in relief. If she understood him correctly, he was telling her that trolls always smelt awful.

Entering the cave as silently and swiftly as they could, Mai continued to follow Jake. He didn't know where he was going, but he'd told her earlier that one of the old men from the village had heard stories as a child about the way trolls live. He'd then passed the information on in the hope that it helped them to navigate their way through the mountain.

So far, so good.

The entrance to the cave was faintly lit by the thankfully strong daylight, enough for Mai to see that the opening appeared empty. There were two tunnels she could see leading off in either direction. She knew this meant that they'd have to go deeper to explore, which wasn't something she was excited about. Reminding herself for the umpteenth time that she was a freaking water *dragon*, Mai squared her shoulders and kept her eyes and ears open.

She faintly heard the muffled sound of someone crying. Tugging on Jake's arm, she drew his attention to the place she thought the sound was emanating from. He nodded, having heard the same thing, tilting his head in the direction Mai had indicated. She nodded and they took the doorway to the right.

The smell became stronger and Mai felt her stomach churn with the odor. Whatever it was that caused trolls to smell that way was certainly unique, but not in a good way.

The ground became rougher the further they went and the ceiling extended higher above them. Mai wondered just how big trolls were and wasn't excited about the possibility of finding out. Suddenly, they emerged into a large open area lit with the faint glow of strange green lanterns along the wall. She wasn't sure what the light was from, but it definitely wasn't coming from a normal fire.

Mai stopped, choking back a gasp, pointing when Jake looked at her sharply. He followed her outstretched arm, then had to hold back an exclamation of his own.

Tucked into the far end of the room, surrounded by what appeared to be a heap of old bones and garbage, was a small cage. It hardly looked big enough for two people but inside it, they could clearly make out the slumped forms of several individuals. At first, Mai thought they were all dead, but then she again heard someone crying, which was definitely originating from the cage itself. Searching the room they saw no one else, so they crept forward cautiously. By the time they reached the small prison, the noise had stopped. Mai knelt down, touching the shoulder of the person closest to her. Their skin was warm, but felt damp, as if they'd been dunked in water. She felt the person move slightly underneath her hand and quickly pulled it back. They sat up, looking at her with a defeated and fearful expression until hope dawned at her prescence.

"Hvem er du?"

The voice hardly made a whisper and sounded so young that Mai's heart cracked open with pain. The face belonged to a small boy with white-blond hair, which was now extremely dirty and caked with mud, but still somehow shone in the dim green light. Not trusting herself to speak, Mai nodded with a lump in her throat before looking at Jake.

"What should we do?" Mai mouthed the words quietly, still not making any sound.

Jake had fire shimmering in his eyes and Mai knew that he was far from being immobilized by heartbreak. Instead, he was ready for battle. She watched as he took a quick look around the room and at the cage, then held up his hand for her to back up, which she did.

As Mai watched, he transformed into a dragon and grabbed a firm hold of the door in his strong jaws and yanked, tearing it off its hinges in one smooth motion. Mai waited until he'd put the door down on the floor, being careful to make as little noise as possible, then she entered the cage and touched each of the bodies that she saw, six in total. One by one the children roused. While they appeared thin and terrified, Mai was relieved to discover that none of them seemed to be seriously injured, or even particularly surprised or frightened by the sight of a dragon in the cave.

The children moved slowly, their muscles cramped from being kept in such a small space without moving. Mai helped them as much as she could, trying to encourage them to hurry. She continued to look nervously over her shoulder with a feeling of impending doom, but all her efforts didn't help.

Suddenly, the thud of heavy footsteps reverberated off the walls as something large lumbered down the hall from the opposite side. Mai froze, looking at Jake with alarm. Still in dragon form, Jake motioned for her to go in front of him. Most of the kids were now safely out of the cage but Mai grabbed the last one, a child who looked to be about four, and lifted her over her shoulder while shooing the others to move faster in front of her. One of the older girls, who appeared to be about the same age as Aud, took the lead. The other children followed her as Mai brought up the rear, still trying to push them to move faster into the light of the entrance.

They'd almost reached the doorway when Mai smelled the foul odour of troll intensify. At the same moment, she heard something cry out with a guttural, rasping screech. She put the child down, pushing them behind her protectively as she turned around to face the noise. Jake stood in front of her in dragon form, looking impressive with his golden brown scales shimmering in the dull light, his tail twitching irritably like a cat about to pounce. The troll stopped a few feet from him and roared again.

Mai shuddered at her first sight of its disgusting green and brown teeth through which saliva spewed. While she had no idea what the troll was saying as it bellowed, she could guess it wasn't a happy greeting, as they watched their winter meal exiting the storage room right in front of them.

Mai knew that they'd have to fight if they wanted to escape. She glanced at the kids behind her, relieved to see that they'd now reached the mouth of the cave and were helping each other pick their way down the steps to the outside world. Mai backed up, guarding their retreat, then stood her ground a few feet behind Jake.

"How many do you think there are?" she asked, not even trying to be quiet now. "Should I change too?"

Jake kept his eyes on the troll, watching for movement.

"Usually there are at least two trolls, but less than five. They live in small family units, since they can't even get along with each other without trying to kill each other. Units are usually a mother and son, or a father and daughter."

Mai nodded resolutely. "Check. So what do you think this one is?"

Mai couldn't tell from the body shape, although it was wearing only a pair of pants, which made her suspect male, if the pants covered the same parts as they would on a human. It seemed to be youngish one, if she could go by its hair color, which was a muddy brown.

Jake shook his head, not looking away from the oncoming threat.

"Male, maybe. It's the females you really have to watch, like with most species." He briefly glanced over his shoulder at her and she could see a glimmer of humor in his eyes.

She snorted, her mood lifting slightly. Just then, the troll rushed at Jake, obviously thinking he was distracted and ready to be taken, but then Jake ducked and the troll tripped, flying over his head and sprawling on the floor beside Mai.

She took a step back, her heart beating faster as the troll stood up. She watched as it seemed to go up, up, and up, until the troll stood almost nine feet in height with its head nearly touching the roof of the cave. It growled and began to shuffle forward, coming straight at her. As it bent over to crush her with its arms, Mai saw an opening and slid between the troll's dirty, warty knees, turning as she skidded through to kick it square in the backside. At the same moment, she saw another troll enter the room and reach for Jake.

"Jake! Watch out!" Mai shouted out a warning while still lying on the floor, before jumping back to a crouching position.

Jake whipped around, his tail spinning almost the full diameter of the room. Just as the creature lunged at him, Jake roared his own battle cry. Using his massive jaws, he bit down on the troll's arm.

Mai looked away, remembering her own adversary, to see the troll teetering precariously on the edge of the cave's entrance. She wasted no time and quickly changed into the azure dragon form in which she had more strength. She pushed, hard. She watched as the troll fell backward over the ledge then dashed over. Luckily, the children had scrambled out of the way of the falling troll. As she continued to observe the troll, she quickly discovered that the old tales were true. When trolls were exposed to sunlight, they turned to stone. There, at the bottom of the steps, children surrounded the pieces of the troll she'd just pushed.

"Look out!"

Mai shouted at the children, waving for them to get out of the way. While they'd avoided being hit by this troll, she wanted them out of the way in case Jake's battle didn't end as neatly. She wasn't sure if they all understood English, but they could tell from her tone that it was urgent, and she was relieved when the older children moved the younger ones back further out of the fall zone. Turning back to the cave to see what was happening with Jake, Mai found him locked in close combat with the remaining troll. Jake still had his jaws clenched tight around one of the troll's arms, but the troll had the other one around his neck and was squeezing and Jake looked like he was fading.

Frantically, Mai searched the cave for a weapon. She recognized something that looked like a cudgel resting against a wall and went for it. Turning back into human form, she picked it up, then circled around behind the troll. She swung the cudgel at hard as she could at the back of its head. A satisfying crack rang out and the troll went limp, allowing Jake to throw it out of the cave and over the ledge, where it joined the other troll in pieces at the bottom.

Jake examined Mai's appearance with a raised eyebrow and she shrugged. Her clothes hadn't made the transition as nicely as she had, what with all the rolling and fighting, but for the most part, they still covered the important parts of her body.

"What do you think yours are going to look like?" she asked, crossing her arms. "I was skidding on the ground a fair bit you know."

Jake chuckled, the sound a deep purr, then sniffed the air.

"I want you to go and wait with the kids. I'm going to take a quick look through the cave to make sure no one was left behind."

Mai hesitated, but Jake shook his head, dismissing her concern.

"It's fine. I don't smell the stench anymore, and if there were more trolls, they'd already have joined the battle. Trolls might be slow and stupid, but they never turn down the chance to fight."

Mai nodded and reluctantly went to the cave entrance, turning back once more to glare at him warningly. "Hurry up. If you aren't back in five minutes, I'm coming in after you."

Jake blew her an awkward dragon kiss as he lumbered back toward the interior of the cave. Mai picked her way down the steps to meet the dazed children, who swarmed her with hugs the moment she reached them. The youngest child looked as if they were only about four and the oldest was a girl who could only be Aud's friend. She was the first to speak.

"Thank you for saving us. How did you know where to find us? I was sure we were going to die." She spoke English and Mai was impressed by her fluency.

"We got directions from some of the village elders. For the most part, Jake knew what to expect. We were just lucky we were able to get to you in time."

The girl gave Mai another big hug, then stepped back smiling.

"My name is Freya. I can never thank you enough. They were planning to butcher us, and soon, I think. We couldn't understand what they were saying, but when we arrived they were finishing off something else. I think they were arguing over what to do next. They were getting together their tools when you arrived."

Mai let out her breath, sending out a prayer to whatever god had kept the children safe until she and Jake arrived and had given them a sunny day on which to kill the trolls with. If they'd shown up even a day earlier, she wasn't sure if they would have been able to defeat the trolls due to their sheer size. The one she'd killed had been pretty much because of dumb luck and the proximity of the edge of cave, and even the one Jake. Had fought had, in the end, been killed by sunlight. Looking down at her watch, Mai gently shook the kids off.

"I have to go back to check on Jake. He's been gone too long."

Mai headed toward the steps, fear rising in her chest until she saw a slightly tattered and filthy figure emerge from the cave doorway and give her a crooked smile. She exhaled, then waited on the bottom step until he descended the stairs before she jumped into his arms to give him a kiss.

"That wasn't five minutes, you jerk."

Mai punched him harder than she'd intended and winced apologetically, before rubbing the spot for him. "Oops, sorry. You worried me, just a little."

Jake gave her a tender kiss on her forehead, then let her slide down to the ground. They turned to face the kids that they'd so hastily ushered out of the cave.

The children appeared to be in varying degrees of shock. All of them were dirty and bedraggled, but other than the expected emotional trauma they saw on their faces, they seemed to be reasonably healthy. Mai was amazed, based on where they'd found them and the fact that it had been several days since the children had gone missing. Luck had truly been on their side. The children watched Mai and Jake with quiet anticipation.

Mai turned to Jake, moving slightly farther away from the children so that they could speak quietly. "So? What's the plan? We're still a fair distance from town and I'm not sure if they're up for a long trip. Is your phone working?"

Jake took it out of his pocket, looking at it before shaking his head.

"No. I only have one bar and that one keeps flashing in and out."

Mai frowned. The weather was nice and they still had at least a few hours of daylight left. "Is there another way of contacting anyone? Coast guard? Any park rangers or anything?"

Jake shook his head again. "Not that I know of."

Mai glanced at the children again. The older ones didn't look too bad, but the little one didn't look strong enough to make the trip under his own steam.

"I'm worried about the little guy," she said finally. "What if we carried the smaller ones? We could maybe take them on our back as dragons. And that way, it's less likely that anything will disturb us. Do you think it would be too scary for them, after everything they've been through?

Mai bit her lip as she assessed them, but Jake simply shrugged.

"I recognize most of these kids. Many of them have...interesting...family trees of their own. Actually, Freya has another form with wings, so she could likely carry someone as well."

Mai looked back at the girl with surprise. Freya noticed her staring and came closer to them.

"Do you want me to help you? I'm more than willing, if there is something I can do."

Jake smiled, patting her on the back. "It's great to see you safe, Freya. We were just looking at the smaller kids and trying to decide the best way to get everyone home."

Freya laughed. "Of course. Well, I wouldn't worry about scaring them after what they've been through in the last few days. I can carry one and so can Erik, if you need more help."

Freya pointed at a short, awkward looking teen that Mai eyed dubiously. Freya noticed her disbelief and smiled knowingly. "He may not look like much, but he has some dwarf in him, and believe me, he can carry a lot of weight. If they hadn't drugged us with their magic at night, I doubt they'd have been able to take him in the first place."

Mai nodded. It could work. If there was four of them to carry the smaller four, things would be perfect.

"Do you think we can get back today?" Mai asked Jake, remembering how long it had taken them to get there in the first place.

"No, probably not." Jake looked up at the position of the sun. "We'll be lucky to make it back to the cave we stayed at the first night, even if we travel in our stronger forms."

Mai sighed with disappointment, then watched as Jake addressed the kids in Norwegian. They watched him as if they were in the presence of a god, hanging on his every word. When he'd finished speaking, he turned back to Mai.

"I told them we were going to change into another shape and that we'd carry the little ones. They were fine with that. Are you?"

He looked at her with concern. Mai had always hidden her other form from everyone except her closest friends. She didn't want people to know that she was something other than human, but she figured since the children had already seen her shift, it didn't matter now.

Mai stood straighter and brushed her hair off her face. "I'm ready if you are. As long as you're sure it won't upset them, I'm totally okay with it."

Jake put his hand on her arm. "They'll be fine. Things are different up here, as I'm sure you've already noticed. Fairy tales are real life, which means that these kids believe in the good stuff, too."

Mai smiled, having no doubt that Jake was right, and let herself flow into the tingle that she always felt as she transformed shapes. It was both odd and gratifying to hear the little voices gasping in admiration at the sight of her bluish-green scales shimmering in the sun. One little girl ran over, then stopped, shyly holding her hand out, and Mai could see that she was itching to pat her. Mai bent her head, feeling the girl gently touch her then giggle at her own audacity.

Mai knelt down and tilted her head. "It's okay, you can climb up if you want. Just hold on behind my neck so you don't fall off."

The girl looked at Jake, waiting for him to translate. He said a few words that caused the girl to smile broadly at Mai before she climbed up.

"I just told her that she could climb up and to hold tight," Jake explained.

Mai smiled and stood up carefully to allow the girl to maintain a solid grip. Jake spoke to a small boy, who also broke out in a big smile before racing over and climbing Jake like a monkey. Mai waited as the short boy said something to the child that appeared to be the youngest, then helped them climb up onto his back. Although small, Mai noticed that he didn't even move when the boy was settled, appearing to be standing as easily as he had moments before being weighed down. Freya shook out her arms and Mai watched curiously, never having watched someone she didn't know transform. She changed into an eagle-like creature in a quick blur. If Mai hadn't known what was happening, she could have easily convinced herself that the girl had been replaced by the creature in front of her.

Within minutes, all of the children were accounted for and being carried by someone. They had decided to walk, as it was the only way they'd all be able to travel together as a group. Mai would have preferred swimming, but knew it would be hard to keep a small child from falling into the water, and Erik apparently couldn't swim. There was also the little problem of the draugr that had threatened them earlier. Freya elected to fly circles around them, her passenger occasionally shrieking with joy as they scouted ahead to make sure nothing was lurking.

They managed to make it to the caves by nightfall, transforming back into their human forms, then tucking the children away safely for the night. Jake had tried several times to get a signal for his phone, but the land or the service had conspired against him and he hadn't been able to connect. The rocky land surrounding them had taken them back to an earlier time, when communication was via people and not machines.

Mai felt strangely happy. Here she was, cut off and isolated from the world around her, potentially at the mercy of whatever evil beings were waiting in the darkness of this odd place where magic seemed to be everywhere. And all she could think about was how at home and content she felt to be with Jake taking care of these innocent children. For the first time in a long while, Mai felt at peace in the universe.

After they had ensured that the younger children were safe in their cave beds that night, Mai looked at Jake and grabbed his hand, leading him to the entrance. Freya saw her and nodded, turning to Erik and saying something before they turned their backs, positioning themselves protectively around the others.

Jake accepted Mai's hand and followed her, an expression of curiosity on his face. Once outside, he stopped, holding their joined hands closer to his heart. "What is it? Is something wrong, Mai?"

She gave his hand a quick kiss. "No. Nothing's wrong. In fact, that's what I wanted to talk about. For the first time since I woke up in that park in San Francisco, I feel like I have a place where I belong. Look around us, Jake. This is like nothing I've ever known. The land here is strange and scary, and full of monsters. We've faced creatures that I've never even heard of before, let alone seen. I've killed a nyk and a troll, and you argued with a dragur about territorial boundaries. We successfully swam away from a kraken. This last week has been overwhelming and liberating, in so many ways."

Jake looked relieved. "So you aren't upset? You still want to marry me?"

Mai laughed, amused by the fear she heard in his voice.

"Of course I do, you silly man. After all of that? I love you even more than I did when we left your parents' house." Mai blushed, remembering the night before. "Now that you've shown me what *love* is," she said then stopped, clearing her throat awkwardly before continuing. "Well, that's something I'd like to practice a bit more."

She'd been looking down as she spoke, feeling uncomfortable at the admission, but when she looked up to see the fire in his eyes she once again felt the familiar yearning rise up in her abdomen. She had to take a deep breath to expand her suddenly collapsed lungs.

"Thank God!" Jake muttered quietly.

When Mai arched her brow and smirked, she saw it was his turn to have rosy cheeks.

"So what did you want to say? I was seriously worried that you were breaking up with me. I even wouldn't blame you under the circumstances. It's not exactly how I wanted to introduce you to my homeland and my family."

Mai touched a soft but steady hand to his cheek.

"Definitely not. I can't wait to marry you. I can't wait to live my life with you. But have you considered maybe that we could stay here? For a while, at least. Is there a rush to get back to the States?"

Jake's mouth dropped before he closed it again. It took him a moment to speak. "Well, no, not really. I just always assumed that you wanted to go home, I mean, you've lived there for literally centuries. I never thought you'd be interested in staying here." He stopped, then snorted. "I mean, I'm from here, and I've never seriously thought about coming home for more than a visit."

Mai smiled, seeing the small-town boy hiding inside the city-man that she knew.

"What if, though? Like you said, this land is different. Things that no one would believe back home are real and unquestioned here. Those kids should be traumatized forever based on what they just went through, but they mostly just look tired. And the way they completely accepted two dragons and a bird-lady as transportation tells me that there's a level of acceptance here that isn't waiting for us back in San Francisco."

Jake shrugged. "I've honestly never thought about it. I don't know what to say. Are you telling me that you want to stay here, in Norway?"

Mai looked off into the twilight at the sky filled with stars.

"I don't know. I'm just saying we should think about it. We don't have anything to race back to. I'd like to get to know your ancestral land better before we make any hard choices." Looking back at Jake and into his eyes, Mai saw that they'd softened from the fear and confusion he'd felt when she'd first taken his hand and returned to the intense gold that she remembered from their first meeting.

"I love you."

She said the words simply, moving smoothly when he drew her into his arms. They shared a deep, sweet kiss that went on for what could have been seconds or hours before slowly releasing. Faces close together, looking into each other's eyes, Mai felt the peace and feeling of homecoming surround her, and smiled.

Tomorrow, they were going home.

CHAPTER
THIRTEEN

Shortly after lunchtime the next day, they made it back to town to be immediately surrounded by joyous people all speaking at once. While Mai had no idea what they were saying for the most part, she completely understood the sentiment. They'd all changed back into their regular human forms just before they reached town, except for Erik, who of course looked exactly the same. While Mai had felt comfortable being herself around the children, she wasn't sure if she was ready to have everyone in the town know her secret.

Freya had understood. "Aud and I will often go for trips together as ourselves, but it's not something we talk about at school. It's never easy to be different, and some people can be cruel, even here, where so much of this is commonplace."

Mai watched with a lump in her throat as each of the children were scooped up by their parents in various degrees of tears and joy. It had been so long since she'd had that experience herself that she was jealous, at least until she looked over at Jake. Someday, she might have kids that she could pick up and love. The thought hit her like a lightning bolt, overwhelming her with amazement and hope.

Jake's father came out of the crowd to clap him on the shoulder, before gripping it with his large hand, bringing him in for a tight hug then slapping him on the back with a laugh as he let go.

"Good job, son! I knew that you were up for the challenge." Anders turned to Mai and pulled her in for a tight squeeze, knocking the air out of her. "And Mai! You have impressed us all. I'm honored to call you my daughter."

As Anders smiled at her, Mai surprised even herself when she burst into tears, unable to hold back her emotions any longer. She tried to stop crying by wiping the tears away, but they wouldn't stop falling. They continued to build up as the sunny sky began to darken around her.

Jake looked at her with concern before pulling her away from his dad, who was frozen with confusion over what he'd done to cause the meltdown.

"Shhh, Mai, it's okay. Don't cry." Jake wrapped her carefully in his arms, getting wet in the tearful downpour, then kissed her until she stopped.

In a few moments, the warmth of his kiss penetrated her tears and she was able to regain control. Jake took a step back to look at her face, still holding onto her carefully, in case she burst into tears again.

"Are you alright? What happened?"

Mai smiled, tear streaks still shining on her face. Dashing at them with the back of her hand, she laughed weakly and apologized.

"I'm sorry, Jake. I didn't mean to literally rain on the parade here. I think I lost it when your dad said I was his daughter." Mai stopped speaking, her throat getting choked up again, but she was able to regain control by breathing slowly for a moment. "It's just that...I never thought I'd ever hear those words again," she sniffed, opening her eyes wide to try to stop the tears before wiping her nose. "I'm sorry."

Anders smiled with relief, reaching out his hand, which she accepted, squeezing it in an attempt to impress her happiness on him. "You are now. I believe that my wife is waiting eagerly to make it official," he said, adding as he looked at each of them in turn. "Although I have a feeling that you've already made your promises to each other, you'll still have to have the formal services in front of an audience."

Mai's mouth dropped open in surprise at his cheeky words, but this time it was Jake whose face flamed red with embarrassment.

"Dad!" Jake said, his face slack with shock as Anders continued to laugh.

"Oh, hush, you. Time to get home. You need to get cleaned up, then you're coming with me to talk to the men." Anders laughter faded as he turned to gaze solemnly at Mai. "I believe Astrid is waiting to talk to you. Now, the true battle begins."

Mai thought he was joking, but it was hard to tell. Astrid had seemed to be warming up to her before they'd left to find the missing children, but Mai wasn't looking forward to dealing with the last-minute details of planning a wedding even if she wasn't in trouble.

"Yes, sir. Do you know where I could find her?"

Mai figured she may as well face up to her fears and waited as Anders took out his phone to call his wife. After a short conversation, he directed Mai to the seamstress' shop and Jake went with her, leaving the throng of happy townsfolk behind them.

"ARE YOU OKAY?" JAKE spoke quietly, grateful for the chance to be alone with Mai. Ever since they'd arrived in Norway, things had been so rushed. He couldn't wait to start his life with her, but it almost felt as if everyone was deliberately getting in the way of him spending time with his love. He watched as Mai nodded, smiling a little too brightly. He recognized her expression as the one she wore when she wanted to reassure him, but was actually feeling overwhelmed.

"I am, really. My reaction just took me by surprise. It was also right after I'd been thinking about having our own kids, so I got a little more emotional than I normally would have."

Mai had been looking forward at the ground as she spoke, so she didn't notice as Jake tripped on a loose cobblestone until he caught himself. He winced at his clumsiness. It always seemed to happen around her, but he couldn't help being distracted as she gave him a sideways smile.

"Are *you* okay? It looked like you tripped back there."

Jake started to bluster, but gave up and sighed, dropping his shoulders instead while Mai's eyebrow's wrinkled with concern.

"This is a big deal, Mai. Marriage and now maybe kids? I want to marry you and be a dad, I just don't know if I'm ready. What if I screw it up? I've never been responsible for anyone else before. Maybe I'm not mature enough. Maybe I'll be an awful parent."

Jake kept walking, holding her hand without speaking as he remembered the one night they'd had together. It suddenly occurred to him that they hadn't used any kind of protection. A weird feeling settled in his stomach the more he considered how careless they'd been. They could have kids a lot sooner than he was expecting. But instead of feeling scared or rushed, a hope and excitement spread through his chest.

After a few minutes of this contemplative silence, Mai abruptly stopped walking.

"Are we ready for a family of our own? I don't know, Jake, but I think it's something that we'll figure out together as we go. It's not like it's all going to happen overnight, after all. The first step is getting all the formalities out of the way. It'll make your mother happy. Then we can just see what happens next. You're going to be an amazing dad, I know that, so don't even go thinking that you won't be."

Jake looked at her hopefully before he nodded, the fierce expression on her face convincing him that she meant every word.

"Okay. You know that I'd believe anything that you tell me. But, speaking of formalities, did you manage to get in touch with Cat and Vanessa, or Evelyn and Zahara before we left? I forgot to ask."

"I talked to Vanessa and asked her to pass the word on to everyone. We've only been gone a week, but that means that the wedding is in just a few days. I'll try to contact them again when we get back to the house. I'm not sure if they'll be able to make it on such short notice, but I hope so. It's because of them that I even have this life and I can't thank them enough." Mai smiled fondly.

Jake couldn't help thinking about what a crazy road it had been to get to where they were now standing.

"But we should go. Your mom's waiting and while she's been nice to me so far, I don't think I want to make her mad at me," she said, tugging at Jake's hand.

He nodded vigorously. "That's a great idea. She can be pretty scary when she's upset. That's probably where they get the idea that dragons have bad tempers."

Grimacing, Mai shuddered. "Let's go now. I definitely don't want to see that."

JAKE DROPPED MAI OFF in the hands of his impatient mother, receiving orders to meet his father immediately in order for Jake to try on his own wedding outfit. Jake agreed without hesitation and swiftly disappeared down the street, leaving Mai to her soon-to-be mother-in-law's mercy. Luckily, Astrid was so happy to have them back that she seemed softer than the previous time Mai had seen her, so after a quick rinse to remove the layers of grime from the trip, Mai was able to try on her dress without any problems.

The wedding dress was every bit as beautiful as she remembered, and the image of the long-ago dress on the bride she'd seen as a child came to her mind. She stared in awe at her reflection. She looked so different from her normal self, regal, somehow. She wasn't wearing any make up and didn't have her hair done, but it didn't matter. She felt like a bride in this dress and excitement at the idea of walking down an aisle with Jake overcame her. For the first time, it was real. Astrid stood behind her, and Mai caught the shimmer of wet blue eyes in the mirror before Astrid noticed Mai watching her, blinking them away rapidly.

Astrid cleared her throat. "Be careful taking the dress off. You don't want to crush the fabric," she said, brusquely. "I'm going to have a quick word with the seamstress."

Mai nodded respectfully, but smiled inwardly. Maybe Astrid wasn't as icy and unsentimental as she seemed on the outside.

The last few hours of the day passed in a whirl. Astrid had already ensured that the flowers and the food were ready and they stopped by the church to make sure that the preparations were almost complete. Mai could feel herself fading, which Astrid eventually noticed and took pity on her.

"I think we're done for the day. We can go back to the house now and have a light meal, then you should get some rest. You're looking tired from your journey."

Mai nodded sleepily and was relieved when they arrived at the house a few minutes later. Astrid was as efficient as always and had already prepared food, so Mai was able to have a sandwich and make her excuses a few minutes later. Jake and his father hadn't yet returned, so Mai sent a quick group text to her friends, then lay down on the bed in her room and fell asleep almost immediately.

CHAPTER
FOURTEEN

Her dreams were a weird place, filled with many of the things that she'd seen over the previous few days and scary at times. But just when she'd begun to replay the fight with the nyk, she felt a wave of light wash over her and the nyk disappeared. Blinking in the radiance, almost blinded, she saw the glow dampen and watched as a figure emerged.

"Evelyn? Oh my God, is that you? Or is this still a dream?"

Mai recognized her friend as Evelyn stepped out of the light, banishing the darkness of the dream that she'd been having, but Mai remained confused. Evelyn had never appeared in one of her dreams before.

Evelyn laughed, coming forward to take her hand.

"Why are those things mutually exclusive? You know where my powers lie."

It was Mai's turn to laugh, ruefully. "Of course, Evelyn. I forget sometimes. You're a goddess of the dream world, after all. Thank you for coming. Can I help you with something?"

Evelyn smiled. "Oh, please! I'm here because of your big news. Since I discovered who I am last year, I haven't been able to spend as much time with everyone, but I miss you guys a lot. I want to hang out, but other things keep getting in my way. I wanted to give you your wedding present tonight, just in case I'm not there on time."

"A wedding present? Evelyn, you don't need to give me anything. Your good wishes are more than enough."

Evelyn waved her hand dismissively, letting go of Mai's fingers.

"Of course you need a wedding present. It's traditional. I'm going to give you two gifts though, one for you and one for Jake."

Evelyn paused, smiling again but mischievously this time while she made Mai wait. Just as Mai started to feel frustrated, Evelyn took pity and spoke again.

"For you, I've spoken to Robin and he's agreed to let our friends come through Summerland to be here for the wedding."

Mai opened her mouth to thank her, but Evelyn raised her hand again.

"Not yet. The other gift is more complicated, so I can't tell you what it is yet. But rest assured, you and Jake will receive the most precious gift of all shortly after the wedding. You don't have to worry about a thing, because I've pulled a few strings to make sure that everything goes well. Do you understand?"

Mai shook her head. "Not at all, but I guess I'll have to take your word for it, whatever 'it' is."

Evelyn laughed lightly. "Good girl. Now, go back to sleep. I'll sprinkle a little good dream juice on you, to make sure you get a better rest this time. You're going to need all your energy over the next little while."

Mai bowed. "Thank you for everything Evelyn, er, Olukun. Sorry, your new name is still confusing me. I'm looking forward to seeing you again."

Evelyn smiled, waving her hand once before the brilliant light radiated out from her, hiding her from sight within seconds. As Evelyn disappeared, Mai's eyes became heavy again, then she saw nothing as she fell into a deep sleep.

WHEN MAI OPENED HER eyes, she was disoriented at the sight of sun drifting gently through the curtains. It took a minute to remember where she was, then she slowly got out of bed and stood up. She wasn't nearly as sore as she thought she'd be, given everything that they'd been through and done over the previous few days. Her thoughts flashed back to what that *everything* entailed and she flushed. She still couldn't believe that she'd made love to Jake, or that she'd held out against making love for as long as she had. She suddenly realized that her wedding was the next day. That meant that she had all the time in the world ahead of her in which to repeat the experience. She felt her face flush deeper then laughed at her reaction. No one was even in the room with her and she was still embarrassed. It was going to take time to get used to the idea of being man and wife, that was for sure.

Rolling over to grab her phone, she saw several messages from Cat, Vanessa, and Zahara, but none from Evelyn. She was initially disappointed, but then the memory of her dream came flooding back and she nodded. Of course. Evelyn was beyond the need for cell phones for keeping in touch these days. It was hard to reconcile Evelyn's new reality with the same friend who'd previously been so impatient to have a phone when she started driving a car.

Scrolling through the messages, Mai could tell that her friends were excited. They'd already spoken to Evelyn and were arriving later that day. After reading that text, Mai hurried to get her clothes on. She went downstairs, wondering if she'd be in trouble for sleeping so long, but when she came into the kitchen she saw that everyone was still eating breakfast.

When Aud noticed her coming down the stairs, she jumped up and launched at her with a hug the minute Mai got to the landing.

"Woah, there! Thank you, but what's this for?" Mai awkwardly patted Aud's back, confused by the exuberant reaction to her presence.

Aud scowled. "Oh, come on! You know what that's for! It's for being so wonderful and saving my friend's life! I can't ever thank you enough."

Mai swallowed her laughter at Aud's over the top reaction, trying to downplay her role. "It was really your brother that did most of the saving. I just helped a little."

Aud scoffed. "That's not what Freya said. She said that you were amazing. And you killed a troll all by yourself!"

Mai shrugged weakly, uncomfortable with her open adoration. "It was kind of an accident, really. I tripped."

Aud started laughing and Mai joined in, realizing how ridiculous she sounded. After she managed to calm down and take a breath, she backtracked and accepted Aud's thanks.

"Okay, fine. I helped a lot. Honestly, it was just lucky that we got to them before the trolls were ready to eat them. It could have been so different if the village men hadn't known where to send us."

Aud nodded wisely. "And if you hadn't gotten Jake away from the nyk."

Surprised that Aud knew about the nyk, Mai looked at Jake. He smiled sheepishly, scratching the back of his neck as his cheeks became rosy.

"They asked how the trip went, so I told them everything," he said.

Mai choked on her own saliva, causing Jake to leap out of his chair to pat her back.

"Not everything," he leaned over, whispering in her ear, then added aloud. "Are you alright?"

Mai nodded, taking the glass of water that Aud offered her and sipped it until the raw feeling in her throat subsided. "Just choked on my spit is all. Went down the wrong way."

Jake nodded, but she saw the twinkle in his eyes. He knew exactly why she'd choked and was enjoying her discomfort.

Luckily, this time it was Christian who started asking questions, wanting to know more about the fight with the nyk. He ended up being disappointed that the battle hadn't been more epic, but was somewhat mollified on learning that Mai had basically crushed it to death.

"Cool," he said, nodding and pursing his lips in approval. "I'd have liked to see that." Christian then quickly lost interest and left the table, saying something about video games, which left Mai with Aud and Jake.

"Mom said she was going to find some last-minute items for the ceremony, and Dad's out working," said Jake, answering Mai's unspoken question as she sat down.

"The girls got back to me. They said they're coming tonight. Did you talk to any of your friends?"

Jake shrugged. "Just Dustin, but he doesn't have the scratch for a trip. And of course, we can't tell him about Summerland. But he said congrats and that he'd take us for dinner when we get back. I don't really care if anyone else comes. It's more important for you to have your friends here. I already have my entire village."

Mai looked at him, concerned that he was downplaying his disappointment, but he smiled back easily. "Mai, this is a formality. I'm already married to you in my mind and heart, so I don't need anyone other than my family here. You don't have any family except your friends, so you need them here. I think we'll be good even if they're the only ones who can make it out."

Mai sighed, her nerves and excitement combining painfully in her chest.

"I can't believe it's already here. Tomorrow we're getting married."

Aud clapped her hands behind Mai. When Mai turned to look, Aud was twirling in circles while clapping wildly.

"I'm going to have a sister! I'm going to have a sister!"

Aud sung a tuneless song as she spun, causing Mai and Jake to laugh at her childish joy. When she finally tired out and sat down, grinning broadly from ear to ear, they changed the subject to discuss more practical issues.

THE DAY PASSED IN A whirl of responsibilities, which Mai found to be almost more draining and difficult than her experience battling the trolls. She had to remind herself repeatedly that it was only one more day before it would all be over. She also remembered something weird she'd heard as a kid that she only now understood. A wedding day wasn't really a party for the bride or groom, but a sign of the formal union between two family groups. And as such, it wasn't expected to be enjoyable for the couple. Mai had kept this in mind as she followed Astrid around without complaint the entire day. It was only when Mai was allowed to carry her dress home that she felt the spark of joy that she'd hoped to feel when she thought of marrying Jake.

Before she knew it, it was time to meet her friends. Evelyn had given the girls the location where Mai and Jake could expect the gate to be, so they left shortly after supper to greet them. The path to the doorway to Summerland took them past the bench where Jake had taken her on their first day in Norway, where she gratefully stole a quiet moment holding hands with Jake while they waited for their friends to arrive.

It had been so busy that they'd hardly had a chance to be alone since getting back. Mai had a sneaking suspicion that this had probably been by design. It was traditional to keep the bride and groom apart the day before the wedding, according to Aud, and Astrid was nothing if not by the book. Mai knew if it wasn't for his parents wanting to keep her safe and sane so that she showed up at the altar in the morning, they'd have likely kept them apart now as well. They lingered over an increasingly passionate kiss until they heard a familiar voice.

"So, are you guys going to get a room or something? Pulease! Out in public and everything. Right where you eat. Bleh."

Mai jumped up from the bench and threw herself at Vanessa. "You guys made it! I'm so happy to see you all!"

One by one Mai hugged her friends, happy that Cat and Zahara had arrived as well. She felt a twinge of disappointment that Evelyn wasn't there, but understood and had the memory of her dream to give her confidence that she'd see her soon.

"Evelyn?" Mai looked at Cat, not surprised when Cat shook her head.

"She can't come right now, but she said she'd do her best to be there for the service tomorrow, unless she can't get away."

Mai pursed her lips. "I understand. It's not like she's even getting to do what she wants to most days. She's got so much responsibility, I don't know how she's coping with it all."

Cat nodded her head in agreement. "So much for her opening her own business or going to university, right? I'm pretty happy that I got away so lucky in comparison."

Mai snorted. Cat was a full-fledged phoenix who could burn demons to ashes and heal people, while Vanessa could control air magic and turn into a raven. Zahara of course, was a sneaky little fox with earth magic, the cutest and smallest of them all, but by no means the weakest in power. Each one of them knew what it meant to be different and have power that interfered with their life goals. For them to all agree that they'd been given fewer responsibilities simply meant that Evelyn/Olukun bore the weight of the entire world on her shoulders, which kind of sucked.

"Well, hopefully she can make it tomorrow. In the meantime, you guys need to come with us and get ready for bed. The ceremony starts bright and early with a hand-fasting beside the water at dawn. We'll get a break after that until the afternoon, when we'll have the church ceremony, followed by the lantern ceremony at dusk. Then we'll have the dance party!" Mai said the last word with a flourish and Vanessa clapped her hands with approval.

"Great! I'm curious to see if there are any other hot Norwegian guys at this thing. Jake, tell us the truth now. Do you have any hot and *single* friends? Older brother? Cousin?"

Jake chuckled, but just shook his head and didn't answer her question. "Nice to see you again too, Vanessa. Come on, we're staying at my parent's place. They've rearranged my room for you guys to share, but someone will have to sleep on an air mattress. I'll bunk in with my brother for now."

Vanessa and Cat shouted in unison, "Not me!"

Zahara spoke for the first time, as the sisters began to glare at each other with an intensity that Mai had seen before. "I'll sleep on the floor. I'm more comfortable in my fox skin, anyway," she said, giving Jake a quick hug. "It's really nice to see you again, Jake. I didn't get a chance to tell you earlier, but congratulations. I'll follow you and Mai back so that I don't have to listen to those two fight."

Zahara glanced back just in time to see Cat stick out her tongue, but pretended not to see it. "Seriously, they've been at it all day!"

Jake led them the few blocks back to the house and in no time at all, the girls were introduced to everyone and tucked into their lodgings, with Aud over the moon to meet other girls with powers. If Astrid wasn't lucky, she was about to lose her daughter to the other end of the world, Mai thought, watching as Aud hung on Vanessa's every word. Well, maybe it would be a right of passage for every one of the Larsens. Move to America to practice their English and find a mate. Mai smiled at the thought, wondering what the future would hold for her new al-most-sister.

CHAPTER
FIFTEEN

The morning of the wedding began with a quiet knock on the door. To Mai's sleepy surprise, both Aud and Astrid were waiting for her.

"Follow me," said Astrid.

Mai nodded, still too fresh from sleep to ask questions. They led her to the master bathroom in Astrid's room, where she was presented with the sight of a hip-deep bath full of steaming hot water, which even had rose petals floating on top. When Mai looked at the two women blankly, Astrid smiled.

"It's traditional for the bride to be given a cleansing bath by the female relatives of the groom, although nowadays most women choose to wash themselves. We'll leave you to your ablutions and wake your friends to get them ready while you relax. When you're finished, towel-dry your hair then put on the gown that's on the chair."

Bemused, Mai watched as Aud and Astrid bowed gently and closed the door behind them. Moving over to the chair to examine the dress Astrid had indicated, Mai saw a diaphanous white gown composed of layer upon layer of white fabric. Surprised, she lightly touched the soft material. She'd had no idea that Astrid was getting a second gown prepared for her. She left the gown and went over to the tub, inhaling the floral scent of the water before removing her clothing.

Mai sank into the tub and let the essence of roses surround her, muscles slowly relaxing in the warmth and the gentle buffeting of the water around her. For the first time since arriving in Norway, she felt completely relaxed. She drifted in the bath for a long time, until the water began to cool off, and only then did she reluctantly stand up and get out. Her wet hair trailed behind her, almost down to her waist. She dried off, putting the gown on as carefully as though it was made of fragile spider webs.

Mai was pleased to find that it fit her perfectly. While the dress had initially appeared to be practically see-through, she was grateful to find that the many layers of fabric hid everything important. Astrid had left underwear for her just beneath it, but it was more of a full-body slip than what Mai had become used to wearing since she'd been living in this century. In a way, it reminded her more closely of what she'd grown up with, causing a surge of familiarity to lighten her heart.

When she opened the door to the bathroom, Mai stopped abruptly to see Aud waiting on a chair just outside. She stood up, motioning to Mai.

"Come with me. We have to keep you and Jake separated for now, so we need to be quiet." Almost whispering, Aud appeared to be suppressing giggles.

Mai nodded, following her into Aud's room with a half-smile, to find Astrid waiting with hairdressing supplies.

"Please, sit." Astrid said, directing Mai to the chair placed in front of her.

Mai sat and Astrid began to do her hair. Watching in the mirror as Astrid's hands gently styled her hair, she was impressed. That such a no-nonsense woman could be so artistic and gentle was something she hadn't expected. Soon, Mai looked into the mirror at a face she hardly recognized. Her hair was arranged in the style women had worn in her youth; with an intricate topknot and soft pieces falling gracefully beside her face. Astrid had added a light, silvery makeup to complete the image, which had the effect of causing Mai to feel that she resembled a beautiful virgin sacrifice. With a twinge of guilt at the thought that this was no longer true, Mai waited until Astrid had finished to thank her.

"Oh, Astrid. I look beautiful. Thank you so much."

Astrid simply nodded. "You're welcome. Come, it's time now to meet the others. The men will be waiting at the ceremonial venue, but the women will all travel together."

Mai stood from the chair, feeling otherworldly and very different from her normal self with her hair and makeup, walking carefully in the diaphanous dress behind Astrid and Aud. She was worried about catching it on the bannister of the stairs, but when she saw her friends waiting downstairs for her, she forget about that as her breath caught.

"You guys look beautiful!"

Each of her friends was dressed in a simple sheath that Astrid had somehow conjured up, each in a pastel shade that complemented their unique beauty.

"Are you ready?" said Vanessa, smiling at her with suspiciously sparkly eyes.

Mai smiled back. "I've never been more ready to do anything in my life."

The retinue of women walked the short distance toward the water, with Astrid and Aud in the lead. They'd arranged themselves in a small phalanx, with Mai surrounded by the others. Mai wondered if this was traditional for weddings in Norway. She couldn't help but marvel at the sensation of safety and support she felt while surrounded by her friends. After only a few minutes, they arrived at the boardwalk beside the water, at the place Mai had started to think of as her and Jake's spot.

Astrid stopped, gesturing for Mai to stay while Aud continued down the dock, followed by Vanessa, Cat, and Zahara. "This is where you'll wait."

Mai stood at the boardwalk end of the dock as instructed, while Astrid walked to the end and began to sing in Norwegian. Mai was surprised at the beautiful bell-like voice that emerged. As Astrid sang, the other women slowly walked onto the dock and lined the left side, followed by men who passed Mai to line the right. She recognized Anders and Christian, but there were another two men she didn't know, followed at the tail end by Jake. The two lines turned to face each other while Jake positioned himself at the end of the dock, then turned to face her.

Mai moved as if in a dream, passing through the gauntlet of friends and strangers to the end where her prize stood, waiting for her.

Jake was dressed in a golden suit with a long tunic and pants that closely resembled tights, with a golden circlet with a topaz in the center on his head. He looked like a prince, waiting for his princess. Mai walked toward him, her heart close to bursting from joy, and had to hold back tears as he stood with his hand outstretched for her. She was breathing fast with nerves and excitement by the time she reached him and when she finally placed her hand in his, her heart skipped a beat.

At that exact moment, Astrid's song ended and a hush fell over the area. When Mai looked to her left, she saw her friends, noticing absently that gruff Vanessa had tears trickling down her face, while Cat had a look of soft wonder in her eyes. As Mai turned back to Jake, the love in his face almost blinded her. He also appeared to be on the verge of tears.

"Friends and family, we are here today in front of God and all of nature to witness the hand-fasting of Jake and his true love, Mai. They are here with us to pledge their love and to promise forever more to be true to each other. Jake, you may begin."

Astrid stepped to the right as Jake moved into the center of the dock. He spoke with a strong, clear voice that seemed to echo into the silence.

"I've been searching for someone to share in all the joy and sorrow that life can bring. Someone who will delight in my success and hold me in my sorrows. Someone who will build a family with me and walk by my side until death do us part."

Jake took Mai's other hand, his golden eyes melting. "Mai, when we first met, I knew that you were the other half of my soul. It's said that dragons mate for life and after meeting you, I know that saying is true for me. I am so grateful and blessed that you said yes. Will you do me the honor of accepting my hand in marriage, so that we can be bound together?"

Jake still held her hands gently. Mai nodded wordlessly, until Astrid gave her a nudge. "Yes, Jake. I will give you my hand, forever. This I promise you. I will walk this path through life as far as it goes, and always be true to you, through whatever may come. In sickness and health, forever together." Mai heard her voice crack with the tears that she was narrowly holding back and smiled up at him, sharing the love that she saw in his face.

Astrid and Anders stepped forward with a rope made of green vines and flowers and Jake held their joined hands in front of them carefully for his parents to wrap. Gently, his mother and father moved around the couple, wrapping their wrists and arms together so that they were bound tightly together in the middle. When they'd finished, Anders and Astrid held up Mai and Jake's joined hands with a proud smile.

"Behold, our son is joined forever more with his soul-mate, his dragon-bride. God protect anyone who tries to come between them, because it is at the risk of their own life. Mai, welcome to the family, daughter." With his last word, Anders choked up.

He took a deep breath and placed an emerald tiara on the top of Mai's head, which unleashed her tears at last. With their hands joined, Jake gently grasped her chin with his hands and kissed her, absorbing her tears as a rainbow magically filled the sky above them.

Mai could feel the light getting brighter behind her closed eyelids and when she opened them, she saw Evelyn smiling from the other end of the dock. She'd added a touch of light to Mai's unintentional water magic and the day lit up like fire behind them. Still joined with the green rope, Mai and Jake walked back down the row of smiling and tearful guests before arriving at a shaded seating area, where Jake helped her to sit down. He smiled at her in the small enclave of privacy.

———— ⟋⟍⟋ ————

"ARE YOU OKAY?"

Jake spoke the words out of habit, but his heart was quivering in its chest. He was married, he had a wife. It was all real. He didn't know what was written on his face, but whatever it was caused Mai's smile to bloom confidently as she shook her head.

"You're always asking if I'm okay. Do I not seem okay?"

Jake shrugged, lost for words. "Is that a trick question? I'm not even sure if I'm okay. I never expected to be so overwhelmed." He laughed dryly. "It was all I could do not to burst into tears. And I don't do that, like, ever."

Jake was overwhelmed by how intense the experience had been. He'd never expected the power of the hand-fasting ceremony to hit him so hard. He'd watched as a child when other couples had performed them at weddings and had always thought they were kind of silly and old-fashioned. But now that he'd participated in one with his soul-mate, everything was different. He realized that Mai was speaking and came back to the present with a jerk.

"Yes, I'm fine, better than fine. The ceremony was absolutely beautiful. But now what? I wasn't sure what to expect for the hand-fasting, but now that part is over, I'm even more confused as to what happens next."

Jake smiled and held up their joined hands. "Traditionally, we're supposed to spend an hour alone, talking about our plans for the future. In the past, this was sometimes the first time a married couple was allowed to be completely alone without a chaperone." He wiggled his eyebrows at her mischievously. "Obviously, times have changed a little. But that's why we weren't allowed to see each other this morning until the ceremony began. Now that it's over, we'll basically just sit here, tied together while the guests mingle. After the hour has passed, there will be a light lunch. Then after that, we'll have the church ceremony with the signing of papers for legal purposes." Jake sighed, already tired by the intense emotions the day had raised in him. "It's going to be a long day. After the church service, there's more food, then speeches, then we're going to have the lanterns. Then there's a dance."

Mai groaned and closed her eyes.

"That's mostly for the young people, though. The older ones usually leave around nine or ten." Jake said, hoping that they'd be able to leave at nine themselves.

"That does sound like a very long day."

Jake nodded. "Yup. I think the goal is to make us too tired to actually consummate the marriage. Good thing that's not a problem, hey? Hey?" Jake poked her gently in the ribs as he joked weakly, causing Mai to snort.

"And now you're telling dad jokes? We don't even have kids yet. Be careful or we won't, if you keep that up."

Mai smiled up at him and he smiled back. Leaning into each other, their lips met, gentle at first around smiling faces, but the kiss quickly became deeper. It seemed like only minutes, but Jake realized that the hour must have passed, because he was rudely brought back to the present with a knock on the wood-framed pergola that was providing their privacy.

"Guys? It's me, Aud."

"You can come in Aud." Jake answered his sister quietly and she stepped in, bowing her head.

"Mom wanted me to let you know that the luncheon is being served on the picnic tables. Everyone's waiting for you to enter the park before they begin eating."

Jake nodded, standing up carefully so that he wouldn't pull too hard on Mai's arm, still tied to him with silk ribbons of green, gold, and white. Mai stood up awkwardly, the loss of her hand control affecting her balance in the dress that made her look like a goddess. Doing his best to walk beside Mai with his much longer gait, Jake worried as he followed his sister that he'd trip and fall on Mai, injuring her on their wedding day. He took smaller steps deliberately and matched her pace.

EVERYONE WAS GATHERED around as Mai and Jake entered the clearing. Silence fell as the couple walked through the crowd, which caused Mai's chest to tighten with embarrassment. She felt as conspicuous as a flamingo in the forest. It seemed as if there were now double the people that had been present at the hand-fast. She was happy to see that Evelyn was still there sitting with the other girls, smiling beautifully at her and Jake as they walked toward the central raised dais. A path had been cleared down the center, and on the dais were two wicker chairs covered with flowers, like thrones for them to sit on. Mai shyly glanced at the faces around her as she passed, then smiled when everyone in attendance burst into applause. Jake beamed back, holding up their joined hands as they settled into their thrones and faced the crowd.

Food arrived immediately, placed on a small table in front of them. Mai had no appetite and instead of eating she found herself staring at the faces around her. She was curiously numb at the sight of everyone watching her with so much attention, then Anders stood, tapped a microphone, and a hush descended as the cheers and catcalls faded away.

"Thank you everyone for coming to our happy day. We are blessed to present our son and his new wife, Jake and Mai, and wish them many happy years together. Would the happy couple please stand up and take a bow!"

He clapped as Mai and Jake stood and the entire group joined in. Holding their hands up again, Mai for once didn't feel awkward as the focus of attention, giving a slight bow as requested. She looked at her friends who were smiling with tears on their cheeks, then at Jake's family, who were all in a similar state. Well, except for Christian. She almost laughed when she noticed him surreptitiously playing a game on his phone, safely behind his mother's back where she couldn't scold him. This was Mai's family now. She'd been alone for so long, and although she still missed her parents and her aunt, she was home now. All of her loneliness vanished in that instant. When Mai smiled this time, it was a smile of pure joy.

THE REST OF THE DAY passed in a blur. They ate and listened to speeches from people that Mai had never even seen before, some in English and others in Norwegian, but all along a similar vein. She was surprised that all of the people present knew Jake and his family were dragons and couldn't help but feel disoriented by such openness after hiding her secret for so long. Jake had told her that things were different here, but she really hadn't expected them to be quite *this* different.

The food was fantastic, with the most delicious wedding cake in the world. Mai had been proud to wear the gorgeous red dress she'd picked out and did her best not to spill any of the rich food on it. Astrid had somehow slipped her away from everyone before the church service and had completely redressed her and freshened up her makeup. It turned out that Astrid was not just an organizational mastermind, but she was also a wizard at arranging people. The church service had passed quickly, and after they signed all the necessary legal papers, they proceeded back to the water where the lantern ceremony lit up the sky. As they let the lanterns go that night over the cool northern waters, she felt their two cultures join. The final piece clicked. This was what she'd been waiting for.

When they entered their bridal suite at the hotel later that night, Jake carried her in as carefully as though she was made of spun glass. He placed her on the floor gently then shut the door. They stared silently at each other and the room faded behind them into the darkness of night while they fell into each other's eyes and privately affirmed their vows again.

CHAPTER
SIXTEEN

Mai and Jake didn't leave the room for two days. Someone had been thoughtful enough to fill the small fridge with cheese, fruit, and various other tasty snacks, and they also had a full bar with all kinds of beverages to choose from. They had access to room service too, but didn't call anyone until well after lunch the next day, content to stay in each other's arms and speak quietly of their dreams for the future.

Mai had never felt so comfortable in her life. Jake was a living, breathing pillow under her head, which she kept almost constantly tucked into the nook between his chest and arm. She sighed contentedly, playing with the hair on his chest with her right hand. He captured it gently, giving it a kiss.

"What's going through your head now?"

The vibration of his voice travelled through her body. She shivered then shrugged with one arm, trying to put her thoughts into words.

"I never want to leave this room. I mean, I know it's silly, but out there's the world, with decisions and hard things to deal with. It's so nice in here. I just want to stay forever, right here with you, doing nothing."

Jake rubbed her arm with his hand and kissed her forehead. "That sounds nice. Do you think my parents will pay for it?" Jake asked the question innocently, but Mai heard his suppressed laughter, and punched him lightly on the chest in punishment.

"Ouch!" he winced.

Mai leaned over to kiss the spot she'd hardly touched. "Oh you're fine, you big baby."

She gave him a mock glare, which caused him to growl and flip her onto her back. She lay trapped beneath him, looking up at his mock-fierceness, and burst out laughing. Jake pretended to pout, but couldn't hold it and looked back down at her with a smile full of amazement.

"I still can't believe you're real."

Mai quieted, becoming solemn as she looked into his eyes. "I'm real. And so are you. This is really happening." She stopped, wrinkling her brow as she thought.

"What is it?" Jake asked, curiously.

Mai shook her head slowly, still looking distant. "I was just remembering something that Evelyn said in my dream."

Jake continued to look confused, but waited for her to continue.

"She said she had a gift for you, but she didn't give you anything, did she?"

Jake shook his head thoughtfully. "No, I don't think so."

Mai shrugged, trying to brush away the small voice that kept nudging her.

"Oh well, she's become a little cryptic since finding out she's a goddess, so maybe it's something we don't know about. Or maybe it was the rainbow at the wedding."

Mai shrugged off the lingering thought that she was missing something, then looked at the clock on the wall and sighed mournfully. "We probably should get back. I want to spend some time with my girls before they go, and I'm sure your parents will want to spend some time with us before we leave, although it's not like we have any plans to go anywhere yet."

Jake rolled back over and sprawled out flat, his arms spread out wide. "Fine, be an adult," he moaned sadly, then sat up brightly, having remembered something. "Let's see if there's any cake left. I asked my mom to hide some for me. I love cake."

Mai shook her head, chuckling. "Sure. Let's go find you some cake."

IT WAS A SHORT TRIP to the Larsen's house, but the day seemed too bright and harsh in comparison to the soft lighting Mai had become accustomed to over the previous few days. They arrived to cheers and hugs when they got back to the house, which compensated for her disorientation with the real world. Mai was happy to see all of her friends waiting to see them, except Evelyn, who was missing again. Cat explained to Mai that Evelyn was needed in Haiti following a tropical storm.

Mai wasn't surprised, but was disappointed to be missing out on a real visit with her. It seemed to Mai that since they'd returned from Scotland, they'd sort of lost their friend. Even though they all understood how important it was to use their abilities when needed, it wasn't always easy to accept the inconveniences that came with them. Great powers and great responsibility yada, yada, Mai thought, somewhat sourly. She was happy that she had the ability to change shapes and control water, but otherwise wasn't as powerful or needed by others as her friend was, which she felt grateful for each time Evelyn disappeared to help somewhere.

"So, how was it?" Vanessa raised an eyebrow, giving Mai a cheeky smile while she waited for her to answer.

"Um... what?" Mai's face began to burn by the time Cat came to her aid, giving Vanessa a swat on her arm.

"Dude, don't be a jerk!" said Cat, then looked at Mai apologetically. "I'm sorry, my sister's not in full control of her mouth. Please don't answer that."

Zahara laughed at the sisters, raising her hands. "What Cat said. I'm glad you guys got a little alone time. Jake's house is almost as loud and crazy as mine. Quiet is hard to come by there, as well. What are your plans for the next week?"

Mai sighed, her blush receding with the sudden change in topic. She gave Zahara and Cat grateful smiles for the rescue. "Well, we're both hoping to catch up with you guys and hang out before you leave. I haven't done much in the way of touristy stuff myself, so I'd love it if you wanted to join me in exploring where Jake grew up. So far, I've found the area beautiful, even if most of what I saw was during a rescue mission."

"Well, I can think of one place that you guys may like," said Aud, flapping her arms with excitement as she interrupted. "It's where most of the young people in town hang out. It's nothing special compared to San Francisco maybe, but the food is good and the music is loud."

ONCE AGAIN, IT WAS Jake and the ladies out on the town. They left the house behind, walking down the narrow streets toward the restaurant. Vanessa bumped shoulders with Jake as they walked, catching his attention.

"So, stud," Vanessa teased. "What's it like to have a harem?"

Jake's ears began to look suspiciously red and he cleared his throat several times.

"Ummm. Well, ummm." He looked desperately at Mai, who smiled and rolled her eyes at his difficulties finding the right words.

"Down, Vanessa. Give the poor guy a break. This is way too much estrogen for one man after the week we've had."

"Here it is!" Aud pointed at the red door one building over and Jake threw his head back, looking at the sky.

"Oh, thank God!" Jake muttered before he opened the door, allowing them to proceed ahead of him.

They entered into a cafeteria-style restaurant, containing a number of small tables for four and a few booths along a side wall. In one corner, a few flashing video games from the eighties were surrounded by teens, and loud music blared from an old style jukebox. Obviously the music had been updated, as one of the latest pop songs was currently playing.

Mai spotted a large booth that was empty and made a beeline for it. Jake squeezed into the corner beside her, and Cat, Vanessa, and Zahara sat across from them. They waited for the waitress to take their orders, then Cat got right down to the questions Mai knew had been plaguing her since she'd arrived in Norway.

Cat checked over her shoulder to make sure they didn't have an audience before plunging in. "So, spill. I need all the details. You must have been so scared! That's super impressive that the two of you were able to get all the kids back safely, all by yourselves."

Mai squirmed in her chair. She hadn't wanted to examine the details of their rescue mission. So far, the wedding planning, followed by the short honeymoon, had kept her mind off all the conflicting emotions she'd had during their encounter with the trolls. Now everything came rushing back. The new creatures that they'd met, the one that she'd maybe, probably, killed. The trolls and that awful smell.

Mai winced. "It was a lot to deal with. I'm not sure I even know where to start."

Jake rubbed her arm encouragingly. "I can start, if you want," he said, waiting only a second for her smile, before launching into details. "Well, it was pretty much what I'd been expecting. I know that people around these parts are more...erm, open...to the paranormal. And I grew up knowing about some stuff. " Jake shrugged, taking a sip of the coke that the waitress had smoothly placed in front of him. "So it wasn't a huge surprise when we encountered a few creatures. Luckily for me, Mai can be a little territorial and came after me at the first roadblock that popped up, otherwise I'd have been toast."

Mai exhaled sharply. She'd hoped he'd leave that part out, but the look of pride on his face was unmistakable. "I'm glad you're so happy with that. I'm still coping with the fact I could murder someone without even seeing what they were up to." Mai shook her head, rubbing her forehead at the memory.

Zahara blinked. "But, Mai, you're the calmest person I know. If you killed someone or something without waiting, I'm thinking your instincts likely overrode your mind." Zahara reached across the table to pat Mai's hand. "That's usually not a bad thing. Sometimes, our minds get in the way. I like to think I'm a pretty nice person, but if someone I loved was in danger, you better believe I'd be on them faster than you can say 'get out of my way.'"

Mai sighed, looking down. "I get that. I do. But at the same time, I still feel like I've done something awful."

Cat interjected. "Remember when I took on Bathory?"

Mai nodded slowly, having completely forgotten about that. "Yes, I do."

"Remember how I burned her to a crisp? Or what about that creepy English dude with the hot dog truck?"

Mai looked up at the ceiling at the memory. That man had terrified her with his darkness. In fact, if it hadn't been for Cat, Mai would have been dead years ago.

"Yeah, but that's completely different. You knew that those guys were completely evil. I can't see that in auras the way you can." She laughed humorlessly. "Heck, I didn't even give this creature time to show themselves as good or bad."

"Um, hello? Are the lights completely off upstairs?" Vanessa looked at Mai as though she'd gone crazy. "Did Jake not just say that he almost died?"

Jake nodded, looking at the girls seriously. "Yes, I was tied up underwater, unconscious. In fact, it took me most of the day to start feeling better, even after Mai got me out."

Vanessa held her hand out, using Jake as her example. "See? My point exactly. Your fiancé was tied up underwater, unconscious, and wouldn't have been able to breathe if he'd actually been human. You basically took out something that had already proven itself to be bad. If you guys couldn't breathe underwater, Jake wouldn't be here now, even with you killing that thing. So stop feeling all bad and morally corrupt, Mai. It's not worth your time or distress."

Vanessa waited for Mai to answer, glaring fiercely at her from beneath her bangs until Mai's shoulders relaxed and she nodded her head in grudging acceptance.

"Fine, you're completely right, all of you. I'll work harder on convincing myself."

Jake hugged her. "That's my girl." He gave her a big smile then stopped talking as their food orders were placed in front of them, waiting for the waitress to walk away.

"Well, the rest of the trip went a lot more smoothly. After that episode, we kept closer to the water, but then we ran into a draugr."

"What's that?" asked Cat, resting her chin on her hand as she listened.

"It's kind of like a dead person. The one we ran into was the Norwegian version of a sailor zombie. Sometimes they're called a draug, or draugen."

Mai laughed, which caused the others to look at her questioningly.

"This encounter actually made me laugh, even at the time. We'd changed into dragons after the draugr saw us and Jake convinced him it was too late, that he'd already eaten our human selves. Then the draugr got all pissy and basically told us to get off it's hunting ground." Mai's smile didn't leave her face. "You kind of had to be there, but it was pretty funny. Jake's a better actor than I'd given him credit for."

Jake looked at her, his mouth open. "Hey!" he said, before crossing his arms and looking away with a huff, chin pointed into the air away from her.

Everyone at the table laughed, then dug into their food.

THE FOOD WAS GOOD, as Aud had promised, and Mai enjoyed catching up with her friends. While it had only been a few weeks since she'd seen Cat and Vanessa, Zahara was further away and it had been several months since the last time they'd seen each other. They were animatedly discussing the pros and cons of Zahara sneaking into concerts in London as a fox, when Mai suddenly started to feel unwell.

Excusing herself from the table, she headed for the bathroom with as much speed as she could muster. She leaned over the closest sink, feeling perspiration bead on her forehead, accompanied by the impending feeling of doom that always appeared whenever she was nauseated. She managed to hold her food down, but had to take several shallow, panting breaths in a half-crouching position before she felt it was safe to move without losing her lunch. Looking at herself in the mirror, Mai let out a quiet groan.

"I look awful!" she muttered, taking a piece of paper towel and wetting it to dab on her face and the back of her neck. "Maybe no more fries today, hmmm?"

Mai looked at her reflection, happy to see that she looked slightly less like the walking dead, but was confused about what had just happened. Generally, she had a really strong stomach, and she couldn't remember the last time she'd been that close to throwing up. But just as she started to feel less nauseated, she was struck by a deep, aching pain in her lower abdomen, just above the pubic bone, that caused her to double over again, as though she'd been punched. It only lasted about a minute, but felt interminable while it was there. Mai knew that something was happening, but wasn't sure what. Feeling shaky, but not wanting to be alone with whatever was happening, she went back to where her friends were still chatting. Conversation stopped the moment they saw her and Cat stood up first.

"Are you okay, Mai? You don't look at all well," said Cat, as she shook her head slowly.

Mai knew she was examining her with aura vision, as Cat's eyes looked blurry and distant. While that particular skill could sometimes be a little uncomfortable for everyone, Mai was grateful for it today, hoping that Cat could just look at her and tell if something was seriously wrong. At least, she thought she was, until Cat abruptly sat down, silent, but with her eyebrows raised.

"What? What do you see? I just suddenly started to feel awful. Am I dying?" Mai covered her mouth as soon as she'd said the words, her imagination running completely away with her.

Cat emphatically shook her head. "No! No, you aren't dying, not at all. Nothing like that. You aren't sick at all actually. But..."

Cat paused, looking around at everyone, then continued. "Let's go back to the house. I want to tell you what I saw in private, without an audience." Cat looked at the others, her head tilted while she waited for their response.

Zahara shrugged. "The less uncomfortable stuff I know about people, the happier I am. That's kind of my motto."

Vanessa snorted. "Agreed. I think it's on my clan crest. As close as I feel that we are, Mai, I'm good having you dole out personal facts in your own sweet time. That way I don't have to handle all the emotions at once. Does that make me shallow?"

Vanessa bit her lip in mock concern and Jake shook his head.

"Yeah, Vanessa, you're as shallow as the Arctic Ocean." He looked at Cat seriously. "I think that if Mai isn't feeling well, we should go home so she can rest. But Mai, I hope that you'll always tell me everything?"

Mai gave him a reassuring smile. "Of course, I will. But right now I'd like to go lay down. Whatever's going on has made me really tired all of a sudden."

Jake slid her out of the bench then got up, putting his arms around her in a warm, soothing hug before he tucked her arm into his.

"Let's go. Can I hold your arm on the way home? I won't if you don't want me to, but it makes me feel like I could catch you, if you feel like you're going to fall."

Mai looked up at his kind and worried eyes with a smile. "Always."

Vanessa rolled her eyes but couldn't quite suppress a soft smile. Cat and Zahara rolled with the change of plans.

"You go first. We'll follow."

Cat smiled and held the door open, a mysterious smile playing around her lips that made Mai wonder what the heck she'd seen. She had a feeling that whatever it was would change everything.

CHAPTER
SEVENTEEN

By the time Mai and her entourage returned to the house, it was mid-afternoon and the place was empty.

Jake looked around, gesturing toward the living room. "We'll sit here while you and Cat go and upstairs to talk. I'll turn on the TV so you won't be overheard accidentally." He looked down at Mai, reluctantly letting go of her arm. "How are you feeling? Any better?"

Mai tried to smile back at Jake reassuringly, but still felt like something was off. "Yeah. I feel almost normal right now. I haven't got a clue what happened back there, but whatever it is seems to have passed now."

Mai gave him a peck on the cheek, not quite missing Cat standing behind him shaking her head at her answer. Mai stepped back and followed Cat upstairs, nervous but curious as to what she knew. Looking around the room to make sure that it wasn't occupied, Mai closed the door after they'd entered.

"Okay, what is it? My nerves are killing me. If I'm not dying, what happened back there?"

Cat motioned to the bed. "I think we should sit down. I'm worried that you'll fall down when I tell you what I saw."

Mai tilted her head at Cat. "But I'm not dying, right?"

Cat slowly shook her head before she sat down and gestured to the spot beside her. "No....the opposite actually. Seriously, you're going to need to sit for this."

Mai sat slowly, her mind swirling in confusion.

Cat took a deep breath before she let it out with a sigh. She took Mai's hand and patted it gently.

"Mai, the reason you don't feel like yourself is because you kind of aren't....just yourself, anyway."

"What do you mean?" Mai felt herself getting irritated at the cryptic answers but forced herself to stay calm.

"I don't know exactly how to say this so I'll just say it. Mai, I'm pretty sure you're pregnant."

Mai felt her mouth drop open and attempted to shut it, but it fell open again. She tried to ask what, but only a small squeak managed to slip out. Clearing her throat, she tried to speak again.

"What? Are you sure? How can you know?"

Cat shrugged, but a smile crept over her face. "It's what I do, remember? I read auras, and I can tell when people have cancer, or a headache, or no soul. Standard stuff, right?"

Mai nodded, fully aware that Cat was skilled at aura reading. "But how do you know I'm pregnant? That's not really a physically *sick* thing. Is it?"

Mai couldn't stop shaking her head, still unable to believe that she was pregnant after less than a week of having sex.

"When someone's pregnant, I don't see a disturbance in their aura, exactly," Cat explained, stopping to catch her breath again. "What I do see is another aura. Babies are a type of growth after all, but they have their own soul, with their own colors."

Mai looked at her wide-eyed. "You can see a baby?"

She looked down at her still small stomach and gently prodded it in wonder before looking back at Cat.

Cat nodded slowly. "Yes...I can. But it's *babies*, Mai."

Mai felt her head spin and put her hands up to hold it. "What? Babies?"

Cat gave her a small grimace of apology. "Yeah. You've got three tiny auras that I can see, all with different colors."

Mai just looked at her for a minute. "Okay, let me get this straight. Not only am I pregnant, in a ridiculously short time after getting married, but there's also three babies in there and they have different colored auras? What does that even mean?"

Cat tilted her head and shrugged helplessly. "I'm not entirely sure, although I think it means that they'll have different affinities. Like, Vanessa's aura looks purple to me and yours looks blue, while Zahara's is kind of a green. I can't really see mine but I think if I could, it would be gold, orange or red. And Evelyn used to be opalescent, but now she's like a diamond and I can hardly look at her aura, it's so damn bright."

"Well, what color are these ones?"

Cat smiled. "They look to be green, gold, and blue."

Mai started to laugh, then was surprised to feel tears leaking slowly down her cheeks with her laughter.

"Um, can you keep those mostly in? I don't think Astrid wants her house flooded."

Cat looked nervous as the tears started to increase in number. Mai wiped them, but kept laughing. Luckily, the tears stopped, replaced by happiness.

"This is so crazy, Cat. I just got married a few days ago, now I'm having triplets and you're telling me they all have different auras, which most likely means different powers. I may go insane. How am I supposed to handle all of this? I don't have any experience with children, like none. I was an only child and an orphan, for God's sake."

Cat pointed out the obvious. "Well, maybe you didn't have any experience, but you'll certainly be getting some shortly. Whatever else may happen, I know you can handle it. Jake's going to be a great dad and you're going to be a great mom. You'll get through it. And I can't wait to see the babies."

Mai was completely blown away, shocked and confused about how it was possible to become pregnant so fast. It had been only a week since the first time she'd had sex and from what she knew about human pregnancies, most people didn't even know they were pregnant until they were a month or two along. For her to already know she was pregnant had to mean that something weird was happening. Maybe, she thought with a sinking feeling, this wasn't a human pregnancy. After all, she was a dragon and so was her mate. Was it possible that she was having...dragon babies?

Mai looked at Cat, who was still sitting next to her, watching her with a cautious and nervous looking smile.

"Cat, I don't think that this is a normal pregnancy."

Mai stood up, feeling the need to move. She began to pace back and forth in the room, absently touching items on the dresser and bookshelves as she moved.

"What do you mean?" Cat asked.

Mai came closer to her and touched her lower abdomen lightly.

"As a human, there's no way I should be pregnant already. Jake and I weren't...close like that...before the wedding, not really."

Mai blushed as she thought of the one night in the crevice where they'd made their vows under the stars.

"If this was a normal pregnancy, I shouldn't even know for a few more weeks and shouldn't be having any symptoms at all. And there's no way you should already be able to see three auras in there. It's just not possible."

"So what do you think is going on?" Cat asked, before adding, "I'm positive that I can see three little auras in there. I've never been wrong about something like that before."

Mai shook her head, brushing away Cat's tone of indignation.

"No, I believe that you really do see three in there. But what I'm saying is that if this was a human pregnancy, you wouldn't be able to see anything yet. I'm thinking that maybe, just maybe, this could be an actual dragon pregnancy."

Now it was Cat's turn to gape at her, mouth opening and closing without words.

"What?" Cat finally asked, forcing the question out.

Mai shrugged, her arms fluttering helplessly.

"We're both dragons. Maybe dragons do pregnancy differently, but I've got no idea what to expect. I have to share this news with Jake right away, and his family, because I'm going to need a lot of advice. Hopefully, Astrid will be able to tell us what's actually happening and what it all means."

Cat nodded. "That's a good idea. How about I get Jake and bring him up here so that you can tell him alone, before letting everyone else know?"

Mai smiled gratefully. "Thank you."

Cat paused at the doorway, before looking back at Mai with concern.

"Make sure he's sitting down? I've got a feeling he may pass out when you tell him."

Mai snorted at the idea of Jake stretched out on the carpet, passed out like a guy in a sitcom after hearing his wife is pregnant. "Good idea. I'm positive it'll be a bit of shock for him as well."

Mai waited in the room alone for what felt like an eternity, worrying about Jake's reaction. She knew that he wanted to have kids, some day, but wasn't sure he was ready yet, especially after he'd admitted being scared the other day. She wasn't ready at all, especially if there were three kids in there. Maybe three little dragons. She pictured tiny cartoon dragons flying around the house, knocking down vases and books, and smiled. It could be fun, though, if she lived through it.

"Are you alright?" Jake's voice interrupted her reverie with the question that was starting to irritate her and she answered with a snap.

"Yes, already. Can you stop asking me that? I'm starting to feel like I'm dying, the way you ask every time you see me."

Mai felt bad the second she spoke and apologized immediately. "I'm sorry Jake, I know you're worried. I'm fine, I promise. Cat just told me what's happening and I think we need to sit down and talk about it."

Mai sat and patted the place beside her for Jake, who came and sat next to her on the bed with worried puppy dog eyes.

"Jake, you know how much I love you, right?"

His face whitened at her choice of starting words. "Mai..." He spoke with hesitation and Mai gently cupped his cheek, shushing him before he could continue.

"And I know how much you love me. What happened today is still fresh to me and I still don't quite understand how it happened, but Jake, I'm pregnant."

She kept her eyes on his face, her hand feeling the prickle of his five o'clock shadow as she watched him carefully, catching the moment his color drained away completely. He swayed slightly and Mai moved her hand down to steady him by the shoulder.

"Jake, breathe!" Mai ordered.

Mai felt him take a deep breath, but waited until he was ready to speak. They sat in silence for a few moments while Jake watched her with stunned eyes. It seemed like an eternity until he spoke again.

"How?"

Mai almost couldn't hear the faint whisper, but when she did, she just shook her head. "I have no idea. Well, other than the obvious." Mai sighed, then soldiered on. "Are you ready for the rest of it?"

Jake's eyes opened wider. "What do you mean the rest of it? There's more?"

Mai smiled nervously before answering. "Just one more thing, well...two, really. Cat could see three auras, all different colors."

Jake blinked at her several times.

"Three? Three babies?" he said, his voice cracking with emotion.

Mai nodded. "Three babies."

Jake smiled then jumped off the bed. He whooped with joy before picking her up and spinning her around. He twirled her a few times before she started to feel queasy.

"Woah! I'm going to throw up!"

Mai warned him with a half-laugh, mostly joking but also uncertain of the strength of her stomach. Jake let her slide down to regain her footing on the floor, placing a gentle, lingering kiss on the mouth before looking at her in awe.

"We're going to be parents."

He spoke in such a reverent tone that tears sprung into her eyes again.

"Yes, we are. I'm happy, but wasn't expecting this so soon. What are we going to do?"

Mai concentrated on drying her eyes and sat back down on the bed.

Jake sat next to her, tucking her hand into his and holding her close.

"We're going to raise them, of course."

He said it so simply, even though Mai knew nothing about it would be simple. She was pretty sure he didn't understand what worried her the most.

"Jake, while I'm happy we're pregnant, I think we need to be prepared for the fact that this isn't going to be a normal pregnancy."

He looked at her with confusion. "What do you mean? I know that triplets are a higher risk pregnancy, so you'll probably have to be careful."

Mai shook her head. "No....that's not it. I shouldn't even be pregnant yet Jake, not according to human timelines, anyway. We haven't been...together...." she said, blushed, then continued, "for long enough for me to be pregnant yet. Or for Cat to see three auras. I'm wondering if we're having...dragons."

Jake's look of disbelief quickly changed into excitement and he jumped off the bed.

"No way! You really think so? That's amazing! I don't think that's happened in years!"

Mai was surprised to see how excited he was.

"So, you've heard of this before?"

Jake nodded emphatically before doing a little dance."Yes, but according to my parents it's been a really, really long time. My parents are distant cousins and they were both dragons, but other than them having us, there haven't been any dragons born in Norway since Christian. While we don't know about what happens in the rest of the world, dragon births are pretty rare. I think you need to have two dragons or the children usually end up being human. It's like, a recessive gene or something."

Mai thought about Naunet, the water goddess who'd appeared to Mai as a mermaid in her dreams. Naunet had taught her about her dragon form, as well as how to control her powers. Mai remembered her saying how there were so few dragons anymore and that she was the last of the azure ones. She hadn't really thought about the significance back then, but that must mean that dragons had been dying out and not reproducing. If she were to have three more dragons, that could potentially shift the balance, but was that a good thing? Mai looked at Jake's happy face and wondered what would happen, then smiled. There was no way having three children to love could ever be bad.

"Let's tell your parents. If this is so rare, we need to know what they know. I don't even know what it means to be pregnant with a human, let alone dragons. Will I give birth to a baby or a dragon? "

Jake agreed quickly. "They'll be super excited and definitely we need to ask what they know. It'll be wonderful, Mai. No matter what happens, we can handle it together."

Mai smiled. She knew that regardless of what else happened, he'd always be there for her. But now it was time to find out what her in-laws knew about her slightly inhuman pregnancy, and what to expect when one was possibly expecting dragons.

CHAPTER
EIGHTEEN

Jake and Mai crept downstairs, attempting to remain unobserved until they knew who was waiting for them. Luckily, it was just their friends, Aud having left to hang out with her own friends and no one else had returned yet. The moment they saw Jake and Mai, all conversation stopped.

Vanessa spoke first. "So? What's the big news? Miss goody-goody over here wouldn't tell us the big secret. I've got my suspicions, but she wouldn't answer. Jerk." Vanessa glared at Cat, who just shrugged.

"Not my story to tell, big sis, so there. Got to get the details from the dragon's mouth this time."

Vanessa snorted, but appeared to be more curious than angry. Zahara was sitting with her elbows on her knees, leaning forward and obviously waiting for Mai to answer.

"Yes, please. It's killing us!" Zahara said.

Mai smiled and sat next to Jake on the couch. "I'm sure you're suspicious, based on the timing alone, but apparently, we're going to be parents."

Both Zahara and Vanessa spoke at once.

"That's fantastic!"

"How amazing!"

Mai nodded. "Thanks, guys. We're very excited. But," she said, then paused and looked at them seriously. "There's a pretty big *but* this time. It sounds like we're having three babies. And there's also a strong possibility that they're going to be dragons."

Vanessa shrieked. "No way! That's so cool!" She was almost crowing with delight, making Mai chuckle at the strength of her response.

Zahara looked surprised, but just as happy. "That's so wonderful. There can never be too many dragons in the world."

Mai smiled. "Thanks. Now we just have to figure out how to tell Jake's parents. Then we'll need to ask them what it means and what we're supposed to do. Dragons apparently aren't known for reproducing very often, from what Jake's heard."

"Tell Jake's parents what?"

A familiar masculine voice came from the doorway. They all turned in surprise to see Anders and Astrid carrying groceries inside.

"Wow, speak of the devil." Vanessa muttered to Zahara under her breath, while she covered a giggle with her hand and nodded in agreement.

"Mom, Dad," said Jake. "We were waiting for you to get home."

Astrid put two bags on the counter, brushing her ice-blonde hair out of her face.

"You were, were you? Alright, what are you up to? It better not be expensive, Jake Larsen." Astrid answered with the usual suspicion with which the mother of three almost-grown kids approached life on a daily basis.

"Um, maybe you should sit down?"

Jake smiled nervously and gestured at the couches in the living room at the same time that Cat jerked her head to the stairs, giving an intense glare at her sister and Zahara. Getting the not-so-subtle hint, the other girls stood up.

"We're just going to go upstairs and rest. Jet lag." Vanessa smiled graciously at the Larsens, while Cat and Zahara murmured in agreement, before they all bolted up the stairs.

Anders came into the living room with his brow arched questioningly. "Okay, this is going to be expensive, isn't it?"

Jake started to shake his head, then paused, looking to Mai for help, his eyes suddenly going wide with the realization. "Oh, my God, it *is* going to be expensive," he moaned.

Mai laughed at Jake and sat down, patting the couch beside her.

"That depends on us, really. But yes, it could be."

Astrid came over now, finished with groceries and intrigued by the exchange.

"Hmmm, so potentially expensive. And I see that your friends have escaped, so it must be something big and related to family."

Astrid stopped suddenly and sat straight up on the plush sofa, as though she had a rod down her back, and looked at Mai. "Are you pregnant?" she asked, her voice squeaking with excitement.

When Mai nodded, Astrid jumped back up to give her a hug.

Jake's father clapped him on the back. "Well, congratulations! The wedding was just in time apparently. Good job!"

Jake shook his head in denial. "Well, not exactly. You see, we've had a rather old-fashioned relationship almost up until the wedding. So we're shocked that this is even happening."

While Anders looked confused, Astrid nodded her head sagely then stood, going over to the fireplace to take a small decorative box off the shelf before sitting back down beside Mai.

Anders looked at his wife with surprise. "What is it?" he asked. "What's in the box?"

Astrid showed them all at the same time, displaying it in her hand. It wasn't very big, just about the size of a pencil case, but it was a beautiful blue with green engravings on it. What surprised Mai was that it had Chinese characters on it, not standard western ones like she'd expected to see. Astrid opened the box and inside was a folded piece of parchment that looked hundreds of years old. Carefully unfolding it, she handed the paper to Mai.

"Please, read this. It's been waiting for you, I think. My mother gave it to me and her mother gave it to her before that. It's been in our family for a very long time. I was always told to keep it safe until the time arose. When I asked when that time would be, my mother just said that I would know."

Astrid looked at Mai, her eyes sparkling with unshed tears, and gave her a tremulous smile as she waited for Mai to look at the paper.

Mai carefully took the paper, not sure that she should even be handling it due to its age, and examined it carefully. It wasn't a long letter, only a few paragraphs in total. It was written in Mandarin, which Mai found difficult to read because of the shaky handwriting, but she did her best to translate it to read it to the others.

DEAR DRAGON-CHILD,

You are the last of the azure dragons if this box has made it into your hands. As such, you have a great responsibility to balance the elements. You have within you the future of the dragon race. Like the ancestors, you have control over the element of water. You shall birth forth three who will be joined together to fight for the world, a trinity of power who will cleanse the world of evil. You must protect them until they can take up their mantle. Their birth will begin a new journey and help to bring balance to the world. Your journey shall begin in thirty six days from the beginning.

May you live for hundreds of years and be blessed with safety and peace.

MAI LOOKED UP, FEELING as though she'd been lost in another world. The writing had taken her back. While the paper was older than she was now, she knew the author. It was the same as writing she remembered from her childhood, when she'd snooped through her father's papers. She wondered now if he'd known what was coming; that he wouldn't be there for her, that she'd somehow be transported to the future. She'd been so young at the time. Her parents had hidden her dragon from the world around them, and even from her until after they'd died. By the time they'd had been lost in the storm at sea, Mai hadn't even known that she had the ability to become one. And yet, here she was, almost one hundred and fifty years from the time her parents had lived, reading words her father had written to her. She didn't know how she knew it, but she was sure that it was his words that were speaking to her now from the page.

"What is it, Mai?" Jake asked.

Mai smiled at Jake through tears. "My father wrote this."

"What? How's that possible?"

Mai shrugged, letting the paper drift to her lap absently.

"I don't know. But do you remember when I told you that he was a diplomat? He often travelled by sea and had business dealings with other diplomats. During the late 1800s, there were many immigrants coming to San Francisco. It's possible he gave it to someone to bring back to your family, Jake. Or maybe even to one of your ancestors."

Anders shook his head in wonder. "The world is a synchronous place. Sometimes what seems completely unrelated ends up being connected after all. Your father has given you his blessing, Mai, after all these years."

Mai looked at Anders as her face crumpled and tears leaked out, slowly tracking down her cheeks. It was true. She felt as though she had family approval after all, as if her father knew where she was now, and was happy for her. She took a deep breath and willed the tears to evaporate. Mai chose her next words carefully.

"If this is true, and my father wrote this, then he must have been able to see into the future. There's no other way that he could have known about this situation otherwise. He saw the three babies and said that they'll be an important trinity to balance the elements, and the world."

Jake nodded. "It makes sense, Mai. You're part of a powerful group of element-wielding women that have recently balanced evil in another way. Maybe the three of them will be tasked the way you, Cat, Vanessa and Zahara were."

Mai sighed. "Is it wrong that I'm sad for them? That they'll have these powers and be charged to defend others, instead of living a normal, powerless life?"

Astrid smiled at her sympathetically. "That's the mother in you speaking, my dear. That protective feeling often hits right at the start and never leaves. That being said, you'll also raise them so that they know their powers and use them correctly. It's your duty and will be your pride."

Mai bowed her head in agreement. "I will. But I know that they'll never have a normal life because of it. Because of me."

Jake patted her knee. "Hey, cheer up! I never had a normal life. I feel like I turned out okay. I grew up knowing what I was and that my family was different from everyone else. But it's been great, because I was always loved and accepted for myself. We'll do the same for them."

Mai smiled. "Yes, we will." A thought suddenly crossed her mind, making her pause. "What did he mean about thirty-six days from the start?"

Mai looked at Jake and his parents and the same sinking pit in her stomach opened up as she watched Astrid's eyes dart over to Anders then back to Mai.

"Oh, damn." The blood drained from Mai's face and for the first time since she'd felt nauseated at the restaurant, she fainted.

AS MAI SLID OFF THE couch, Jake leapt forward, catching her limp body in his arms. He held her tenderly, anxiously looking at his parents.

"Is she okay? What should I do? Should we call an ambulance?"

"No, son," Astrid chuckled, smoothing out her shirt before looking at him reassuringly. "She's simply fainted from all the excitement, maybe also because of the pregnancy. I remember my first pregnancy with you, dear. I used to go down at the slightest stressor. And having triplets in just over a month takes a lot of her energy, I'm sure. Why don't you take her up to her room, so that she can rest?"

Jake sighed, brushing Mai's hair back off her face, and bent to give her a kiss on the forehead. Poor Mai. It was a lot to handle, all at once. The trip to Norway, meeting his family, getting married, and now finding out she was pregnant with triplets. It was overwhelming for him and he didn't even have any physical symptoms to deal with, on top of everything else. He moved her onto his lap and put both arms underneath her, lifting her up as though she were an infant. He walked up the stairs, his father following silently behind him. Once they arrived at the room, Anders opened the door and Jake deposited Mai onto the bed so gently that it hardly moved. He tucked her in with a duvet, making sure that she looked comfortable, then turned the light off and left the room.

"Now what?" Jake heard his plaintive question as he closed the door and felt like a kid again, asking his dad for help.

Anders smiled, his eyes crinkling with the wisdom that Jake had always respected. "Well, son, now you get to learn how to be a father. There's nothing as rewarding as watching your children grow into good people. And whenever you need help, your mother and I are always here for you."

Jake laughed, hearing it almost turned into a cry as he leaned into his father's broad shoulder. "I love you, Dad. I only hope I can be half the man you are."

Anders patted him on the back, shushing him. "Oh, boy, you're already more than you know. Now, go back in there and wait for your bride to wake up. You've got this."

WHEN MAI OPENED HER eyes, she found herself looking at the ceiling in the room she'd been staying in before the wedding, tucked cozily into bed, surrounded by pillows and with a worried Jake watching from across the room. He was sitting in the chair by the dresser but jumped to his feet when he noticed that her eyes were open.

"Are you feeling better? Can I get you a drink? Something to eat?"

Mai blinked fuzzily at him before smiling and covering her face in embarrassment.

"I'm so sorry. I don't know what happened. One minute I felt fine, then..."

Mai trailed off, her memory of what had triggered her faint suddenly returning. She had to lie back in the bed and look at the ceiling until she started to feel less dizzy.

"Jake, did you speak with your parents after I had my fit of the vapors?"

Jake looked confused. "What?"

Mai sighed. Obviously that wasn't a common saying anymore. "After I fainted, did you guys talk?"

Jake's eyelids flickered and his eyes shifted before he quickly looked back at her.

"Not really, no. Why?"

"Jake, you're an awful liar. What did they say?"

Jake caved quickly, dropping his head and looking away from her.

"Well, it was mostly my mom who talked, but not much, really. She thinks that in thirty-six days we're going to be parents."

"Ugh. That's what I thought the letter meant. I was really hoping it didn't, but I figured I wouldn't be that lucky."

Jake sat beside her on the bed and took her hand. "I'm really sorry. This isn't exactly how I wanted to start our lives together, but at the same time, I'm excited. I've always wanted to have children. I couldn't imagine that without you as their mother."

Mai smiled halfheartedly. "That's nice to hear. I want kids too, but I'm not sure having triplets a month after you find out you're pregnant, immediately after getting married, is something you get used to right away. Did your mother happen to mention whether or not I'm having baby dragon eggs, or baby humans?" Mai shook her head before he could answer. "I can't believe I'm actually hoping I have eggs. Definitely not how I pictured becoming a mother."

Jake exhaled and sat next to her. They looked at each other with matching expressions of disbelief until Mai spoke again.

"Well, I guess we should prepare for this, whatever it is. I'd like to speak to your mother, if you think she'd be willing to talk about this. She's kind of the expert in having dragon children at the moment, possibly the only one alive, from the sounds of it."

Jake stood up. "Yeah, you're right. I'll ask her to come up. Did you want anything while I'm downstairs? A drink? Something to eat?"

Mai started to decline, but at that moment her stomach growled.

"Um, yeah, actually. Can you find me some meat? I'm suddenly ravenous, but specifically for meat." She looked at him with surprise and Jake laughed.

"Sure." He gave her a quick kiss on the forehead before bounding out of the room.

Mai shook her head at his eagerness before turning to look out the window. Less than a month until she became a mother to a prophecy, apparently. Predicted by her father over a hundred years ago. She'd been alone and lonely in the world until recently and now this. She was going to be surrounded by so much family that the thought almost made her nauseated.

No, wait, she thought, bolting straight up in bed and covering her mouth. Luckily, she made it to the unoccupied bathroom in time. Locking the door behind her, she sprawled in front of the toilet and emptied out the small amount of food she'd managed to keep down at the restaurant earlier.

"Okay, so no more fries. Fine. Just try to keep it down in there, okay?"

Mai groaned at her unborn parasites' opinions before standing up gingerly and moving slowly over to the sink. While not a hundred percent, she felt much better already. Weird how it came in waves like that, she thought. Well, at least it's only another month of this. She'd heard horror stories about women throwing up for nine months straight while expecting and was glad of that one small mercy. She wiped her face and rinsed her mouth, before shaking her pale face at herself in the mirror and sighing.

"Yup, we're in this together, that's for sure."

She made sure the bathroom was in the same state as it had been when she'd entered, then returned to her room to lie back down.

She must have dozed off, because the light was different when she next opened her eyes. She saw a plate of sandwiches sitting beside her with a glass of what smelled like iced tea. Hunger pangs stabbed insistently at her and she sat up, thankfully nausea-free. She ate slowly and waited to see what would happen, but had no further return of the violent attack of nausea that had hit her so suddenly earlier.

Once her stomach was satisfied, she sat up and smoothed her hair down before going downstairs to see where the others were. As she'd expected, they were all gathered around the table downstairs. The smell of warm food assailed her suddenly too-sensitive nose and she felt her stomach lurch once, before grudgingly settling down as she breathed through the discomfort. When the others noticed her, she blushed, not enjoying the spotlight that seemed to be shining on her all the time.

"How are you feeling?" Astrid spoke first.

Mai could see that she was genuinely concerned. It felt nice to have that motherly warmth directed at her.

"Better, thanks. I have a lot of questions I'm hoping you can answer. You know more about this than anyone else I can think of."

Astrid inclined her head. "Of course. Why don't we sit down after supper and talk more? There are a few things that you should know, as well as some things you'll need to prepare for the upcoming events."

"Thanks. Thank you for everything Astrid, and you too, Anders. Thank you both for welcoming me into your home and raising such an amazing son. I can only hope that I do as good a job with these kids as you have with yours."

Anders beamed at her before returning to his food, but Mai watch as Astrid became teary before waving away her thanks.

"You'll do just fine. Now, sit and eat something. You'll need your energy for the coming days."

Mai almost deferred until a growl from her stomach hit her again.

"I don't mind if I do. It smells wonderful."

CHAPTER NINETEEN

The next few days passed in a blur. Mai began to feel that she was living life in fast forward with all of the changes happening to her body. She quickly lost any hint of a waistline and felt constant uncomfortable stretching sensations in her pelvis and her breasts. It was, for all intents and purposes, a normal pregnancy, just at ten times the normal speed. This meant that she was tired almost all the time, that everything hurt, and that while her relationship with Jake got stronger, her love life was placed on hold for the foreseeable future.

She didn't have the energy for a replay of their honeymoon, and Jake was so worried about hurting her that he'd choose to rub her feet or back instead of giving her the passionate kisses she'd grown attached to. She was grateful and too tired to worry much about the lack of passion. When she did complain about feeling unattractive one day during a weak moment, Jake had emphatically reassured her that it wasn't the case. Mai remained content after that, knowing that this would only be a temporary lull in their physical activity, based on the way he'd continued to watch her with his molten gaze whenever he'd given her the chaste rubs that she'd come to enjoy on her aching body.

Astrid had filled her in on what to expect in the pregnancy. As Mai had suspected, she was going to be having baby dragon eggs. It made sense. Having eggs would likely be a lot easier than having three fully grown human babies after a six week gestation. The part that worried her the most as Astrid had explained all of the details about what to expect was the obvious fact that this would have to be a home birth.

Mai knew many women who'd died in childbirth. She'd been happy when she'd found out how rare it was for that to happen now and had been ecstatic to learn about epidurals. But the minute Astrid had explained what was going to happen to her, the painless hospital bubble had been firmly burst. Obviously, she couldn't give birth to three eggs in a traditional hospital or there was the very real possibility that she'd be locked up in a zoo, or viewed as a science experiment. Astrid had reassured her that she knew a midwife, the same one who'd delivered her children, who would be able to come soon to meet with Mai and answer her questions.

And this was why, three days after finding out that she'd be a dragon mother in only a few weeks, Mai and Astrid were scoping out locations for her to lay her eggs. It felt bizarre, like something out of the sci-fi movies that she'd come to love watching since being with Jake. But at the same time, it felt so incredibly domestic and normal. Astrid knew the local real estate well and had a few places for Mai and Jake to look at, but it really came down to where Mai would be the most comfortable.

She fell in love with a small two-bedroom cottage near the bridge where they'd been married. Within a few days, they'd moved the sparse belongings they'd brought with them from

San Francisco or received at the wedding to the already fully furnished place. Their friends had left, going back through the Summerland gate with promises to come back as soon as the babies hatched. Mai had been sad but also excited to see them leave, knowing that she was one step closer to a new family life and wanting to have fewer people around her at the time of delivery. If it was a delivery. Maybe she should call it a laying? Mai shook her head, confused about what to expect and how to refer the upcoming event.

Astrid had warned her that her pregnancy would be far shorter than if she was having a human baby. Yet even with that knowledge, Mai was having a hard time with the physical changes she was experiencing. She had intense bouts of nausea and vomiting, but randomly, and not always at the same time during the day. Her abdomen quickly enlarged to the point where she could barely see her toes and her ankles were swollen within a few weeks.

Along with her increasing size, which she'd expected, she was also breaking out like crazy, which was arguably the hardest part for her. It was one thing to feel like crap, but looking like crappier pizza version of herself on top of everything else was a cruel joke. The midwife, Brunhild, was knowledgeable and reassuring, which helped allay some of Mai's concerns, but she knew she wouldn't be able to relax until the pregnancy and delivery were over. Mai found herself spending as much of her time as she could in her dragon form, which was the only way she could begin to feel even slightly comfortable.

So this was why, only weeks after the wedding, Mai found herself feeling the urge to make herself a cozy nest in the true meaning of the word. Jake walked in one day after fishing with his father and brother to the sight of Mai, in her dragon form, making a blanket fort in a corner.

"Hey, honey, um, whatcha doin'?"

Jake stopped in the doorway of the bedroom and cocked his head curiously, waiting for her response. Mai looked over at him dismissively as she continued to arrange the blankets.

"I need to get everything ready. I don't know why, but it feels like time for me to get everything in place."

Jake nodded his head a few times, not saying anything as he let her words and the scene in front of him sink in. Mai continued to gather all the blankets and cushions that she'd been able to find in the house and had by this time made a cozy space about six feet in diameter. It contained most of the cushions, which had been placed on the floor, entwined with some softer, velvety blankets that she'd found in a closet. They smelled a little like mothballs, but she felt that with some fresh grass and flowers they'd lose that scent quickly. She hummed tunelessly to herself and felt sudden intense pressure in her lower abdomen.

"Oh!" Mai started, her hands reaching down to hold herself, discovering that her lower abdomen was as hard as a rock.

Jake was beside her instantly. The look on his face was equal parts excitement and fear. "What is it? Are you okay? Is it the babies?"

Mai looked at him calmly, almost absently. "It's time. Go get your mother and the midwife. I need to finish this. Oh, and I need some grass and flowers. Ask your mom if you don't know what to get. She'll know." Mai smiled at him before patting his cheek and turning back to continue working on her nest.

It was odd, she thought, how calm she felt right now. She wasn't looking forward to the discomfort, but felt ready for it. She wanted to meet her babies, and thought, no she *knew*, that everything was going to be just fine. Mai felt a peace descend on her that was strangely like distant memories of her mother's warm embrace and knew that this had all been foretold long before she'd been born. Therefore, everything would work out, because it was much, much bigger than her.

Stepping back to look at her nest from the outside, Mai nodded with satisfaction. It was perfect. She stepped into the nest and sat right in the middle, after feeling the need to turn clockwise, then counterclockwise three times. Hmmm, she thought, maybe I have a little cat in me as well. She smiled at the thought before curling up into a round dragon ball, feeling the tingle of anticipation ripple as she settled into her azure shape and closed her eyes, falling asleep immediately.

Mai slept until a feeling of intense pressure in her pelvis woke her up. As she was still in dragon form, she wouldn't have described it as a pain exactly, more like an ache, or an expanding cramping that slowly took over her consciousness. She felt her tongue loll out of her mouth as she took shorter breaths, relaxing after a minute or so had passed and the intensity of the sensation had eased. She sat up a little straighter and looked around the room. The light was entering from a different angle now, so she knew it must be hours later. She looked over to the bed which was now almost bare of coverings and saw Jake, fast asleep.

Mai smiled. "Hey. When did you get here? I must have dozed off."

Jake sat up, bolting upright as though an alarm had gone off.

"What? Mai? Do you need help? Should I get Brunhild?"

Mai flicked her tail once. "No, I'm fine. I just had some discomfort, but it's gone now."

Jake stood up, moving closer to the door with a nervous expression.

"I'll go and get her. She asked me to when you woke up. I'll be right back, okay?"

Mai smiled before putting her head back on her side and closing her eyes. She didn't fall back asleep though. She once more started to feel the same tensing and deep ache that had woken her up, again instinctively panting to get through it. She was completely within the moment and the feeling, not realizing until it had passed again that she had an audience.

Brunhild stood near the nest with an expression of approval. She waited until Mai sat back up again before she spoke. "I see that the birthing has begun. You're doing well, my child. Now all we need to do is wait. Much like with humans, the body almost always will take care of everything if we leave it alone. Of course, sometimes things don't go well, but that's what I'm here for. Are you hungry? Or thirsty?"

Mai sighed and thought for a moment, before shaking her head. "No, just having the most intense discomfort I've ever had. How long will it last?"

She hoped it wouldn't be long, but Brunhild just shrugged.

"It could be a few minutes or a few days. Everyone is different. And because you have three, it may take longer. The first usually is the longest, but sometimes the others take their time as well."

Mai sighed, sinking back down into the nest. While not the answer she'd hoped for, it was what she'd expected to hear.

The rest of the night passed in the same fashion. Every few minutes, Mai would feel the intense pressure and cramping, followed by a few moments of relief. After awhile, the relief between contractions wasn't enough, and she started to feel an intense burning down below.

"Brunhild, something's changing. What's happening?" Mai looked at the midwife anxiously, but when she still appeared calm, she relaxed back into Jake, who continued stroking her back gently.

"Let me see, hmmmm?" Brunhild went to examine her.

Jake looked away, not wanting to see. The midwife clucked a little then looked up with a twinkle, meeting Mai's worried and tired gaze.

"I think you're ready to become a mother, yes?"

Mai let her breath out with relief and felt some of her anxiety leave, now that the moment was finally here. "Yes, I'm ready. Now what?"

Brunhild stepped back and came around to face her. "The babes will take turns, but once the first comes out, the others often follow quickly. All you need to do is push when you feel that you can't *not* push. Do you understand?"

Mai closed her eyes and nodded.

"Perfect. Now, we wait until that happens. I'm here if you need assistance, but I anticipate that in your dragon form you'll be quite capable of doing this on your own. Jake?"

He looked at the midwife, fear in his eyes. "Yes? What can I do?"

Brunhild smiled. "You can do whatever Mai would like. For now, you can do what you're doing until she decides that she doesn't want that anymore."

Jake's face was pale, but his mouth was firmly set. Mai could see that he was still worried, although having a purpose appeared to have steadied him.

Mai had just a few moments reprieve until the pressure came back, but this time she felt the urge to bear down, with the overwhelming urge to scream escaping her as she did so. She felt the smooth, hard edge of an egg pass through her body, leaving her with a feeling of emptiness that was quickly filled, then repeated twice more within seconds. There was no waiting for these younglings. They came out quickly, in single file and without pause, until she was spent, laying on her nest of cushions and blankets with the smell of summer flowers in her nose. Jake had done well with the flowers.

The room filled with cheers and Mai heard Astrid come back in. She could hardly open her eyes she was so tired, but she still managed to smile at Jake. He gave her a kiss on the forehead then a hug that couldn't quite reach around her large body, before he bent down to examine his young.

Mai opened her eyes once more, watching as he crooned over a small pile of eggs, three beautiful eggs in metallic shades of green, blue, and gold. Covered cozily in a velvet throw, they looked almost like Easter eggs, Mai thought with amusement. She closed her eyes again and slept.

CHAPTER
TWENTY

M ai opened her eyes to sun streaming through an open window and birdsong filling the air. She stretched instinctively, sore in places that she hadn't expected to be sore, then her memory came flooding back. She sat up, noticing that sometime during the night she'd returned to her human form and that someone, most likely Jake, had redressed her in her house coat. Looking around in panic, she sighed in relief when she saw the eggs next to her in the nest then curled her body around them protectively. She stayed in her human shape, content to just stare at the eggs in awe. They were the most beautiful things she'd ever seen. Rich, shiny, metallic jewel tones. And inside them, her heart rested, waiting to wake up.

A quiet knock broke the silence and Mai looked at the door to see the elegant shape of her mother-in-law entering the room.

"How are you feeling today, dear?" Astrid spoke quietly, but not without concern.

"I'm fine."

Mai looked at the eggs again with wonder, and Astrid smiled, with fondness this time.

"I remember that feeling. When you see your child for the first time. There's nothing quite like that moment. And when they hatch, things will never be this quiet, ever again." Astrid shook her head and laughed ruefully.

Mai looked at her, eyebrows knitting together in worry as she again wondered what she'd gotten herself into.

"Don't worry Mai, I'll help. Aud will be happy to help as well." Astrid laughed again. "We most likely won't get much help from Anders or Christian, but that's not really what I expect from them. Jake will be good, though. He's always loved children and babysat often when he was growing up."

Mai nodded, grateful she'd be able to count on the help of other women, as she'd heard that newborns were exhausting. She had three now and was pretty sure that meant life would be three times as exhausting. Unless it was a factor thing, then it would be nine times more exhausting. She groaned at the thought.

"How long until they hatch? Will it be long?"

Astrid shook her head. "No, likely only a day or so. Now that they're out, the rest is fast. In the meantime, we need to get you ready. They'll be hungry and very busy. Dragon babies are a handful. And I've only ever had one at a time!"

Astrid spoke while she continued moving around the room, tidying and freshening as she went. Mai watched, feeling the small amount of energy she had leaving her as Astrid cleaned. Mai was eager to meet her babies, but afraid of how she'd cope, given this kind of reassurance.

As Astrid had promised, it wasn't long before she found out. The very next day, she felt the crack of a shell as she rested on top of the eggs. She leaned back into Jake, who'd been helping keep them warm, and they sat and watched as the three small dragons hatched. It began slowly at first, with cracks appearing in the shells, followed by bigger and deeper grooves. The gold egg went first, with a piece of shell flying several inches into the air when a tiny clawed foot punched its way out. It was followed quickly by another foot, then a wing, and lastly a small head with a pointed chin and topaz eyes that peaked out curiously.

Mai felt her heart explode with love.

"Oh! Jake! Look at it!"

Jake smiled and grabbed her hand, lacing his fingers through hers and squeezing. The green egg followed next, with the blue one last, seeming to almost flow gently out into the world. In only moments, Jake and Mai found themselves in a cozy nest with three two foot long dragons that were crawling all over them and each other.

Jake laughed joyfully and Mai joined in. The dragons were almost like puppies in the way they gamboled over everything. Mai felt happier than she'd ever been. She'd thought that her wedding had been the happiest moment of her life, but that was before this.

"We did it Jake. We're parents." Mai whispered, almost reverently. "Now what?"

Jake kissed her forehead and whispered back, trying not to disturb the babies.

"Now we have to feed and raise these little guys. Mom said she'd help, right?"

He went from reassuring Mai to sounding nervous and Mai found herself laughing again.

"Yes, you big wuss. And she volunteered your sister as well. I guess we're staying here for now. The decision seems to have been made for us."

Jake smiled back at her with a mixture of embarrassment and uncertainty. "Um, yeah, I think so. Unless you don't want to?"

Mai shook her head, smiling back without hesitation.

"Oh, heck no. I'm going to take as much help as I can. I'm not completely delusional. We'll need a lot of help with three kids. I'm staying until they're a little older, at the bare minimum a year. But maybe it's okay if we stay longer too. Like maybe when they're ready to graduate."

Jake looked at her with confusion. "What do you mean?"

Mai shrugged. "Well, it's not like either of us has family back in San Francisco. I may have grown up there, but it's changed from my childhood into a place that doesn't really feel like home. It would be nice to raise the kids near your family, so that they have the connection that I've been missing for so long."

Jake held her hands and looked at her intently for several minutes, before he finally sighed. "I didn't want to influence you, but I'm glad you want to stay here. I can't think of anywhere else I'd rather raise my kids than the village I grew up in. They'll learn the old ways from the elders of the village and grow up loved and protected by everyone."

Mai felt tears well in her eyes as she thought about the difference between her childhood and what her children would experience.

"I'd really like that, especially if they're going to have to save the world someday. It'll be good if they learn as much as they can and grow into their powers in a place where they won't be freaks."

Jake nodded. "The old ways are alive and well here. Of course, it won't be for awhile, but it's nice that if we lose a dragon, which I'm sure will happen at least once, they won't end up in a zoo or a science lab somewhere."

Mai grimaced. "I hadn't even thought of that. But yeah, I guess that's something that could happen with three busy kids. Oh dear. We should have a contingency plan for that, just in case."

As they talked and planned the future of their little dragons, a thought crossed her mind. "We need names. Jake, I never considered that! But I'm not sure what we have here. Are they girls or boys?"

Jake raised his eyebrows. "I don't know. I've never learned how to gender a baby dragon. But do we care? I mean, boy or girl, it doesn't matter to me. Any names that you like in particular?"

Mai thought for a moment. "Well, we have a water, an earth, and a fire, if Cat is correct. Maybe if we name them for their natures?"

"Sure." Jake agreed. "Although I'd like to name at least one Freya."

"That's fine with me, but maybe let's wait until we see which one's a girl? That's not a name I want for a boy."

Jake laughed. "Of course! There's no rush, other than people bugging us for names. It's not like they'll answer to us yet anyway."

Mai sighed and leaned back into his arms.

"Jake, I love you. I'm so glad we met when we did. And I'm so happy to be the mother of your dragons."

He squeezed her back tightly and they sat together, in awe of the new life that had brightened their lives.

CHAPTER
TWENTY ONE

The following days and months passed in a blur of sleep deprivation and tears. Some tears were even from the children, but most came from Mai and Jake being completely overwhelmed with the challenges brought by their offspring. As they'd expected, they had needed a village. Baby dragons may start out small, but they didn't stay put for long. Mai and Jake had a hard time keeping up with them most of the time.

It turned out that they had two girls and a boy. The boy was a water power, so he'd been named Peter, after Cat's father, a man they both respected who had water gifts of his own. The girls were earth and fire, so they'd been named Freya and Gaia to match their abilities. Each child lived up to their elemental nature in more ways than one, and before long, fires had to be put out, or water drained from one room or another. In human form, they'd become active and loveable toddlers in what felt like the blink of an eye. Mai couldn't believe how fast time was moving.

Although there was no such thing as sleep most nights for her, Mai wouldn't have changed any of it for the world. Which was why, tired from another night of next to no sleep, she was surprised to walk into the kitchen of their small house to see Evelyn sitting at the table with a cup of coffee, waiting for her.

"Evelyn? Oh my god! When did you get here? It's so good to see you!"

Mai rushed to give her friend a hug, gratified to feel that she was hugged back every bit as tightly. She stepped back to look at Evelyn, realizing quickly that she looked every bit as tired as Mai felt.

"Is something wrong? You look, well, you look great as always, but kind of... tired. How is everything?"

Evelyn smiled at Mai, but it didn't reach her eyes.

"I'm fine, Mai. Thanks for asking. But yeah, I'm sure you know that things have been a little tough lately. The world isn't a safe place most of the time, but it seems like things are getting worse. Or maybe I just feel it more, now that I've got more jacked up powers."

Mai nodded. Before Evelyn had regained some of her memories and the powers that went along with them, she'd been a relatively normal teenage girl with a small amount of precognitive ability. But since they had returned from Scotland, she'd been overwhelmed with the need to help those who suffered. And because she could feel the emotions of others, Mai knew that Evelyn felt all their pain as well.

"Is there anything I can do?" Mai asked.

Evelyn shook her head, smiling gratefully.

"Thanks, Mai. The only thing I want is for you and Jake to focus on raising your children to be strong and kind. That's the best gift that anyone can give the world."

"I'll do my best," Mai promised. "So, when did you get here? How long are you going to stay?"

Evelyn smiled, raising a shoulder diffidently. "I just got here about ten minutes ago. I was making sure that things were ready for your other guests."

Mai blinked. "Other guests?" Mai gasped, "Did you bring the girls?"

Evelyn nodded, smiling smugly. "Maybe."

Mai shrieked and clapped her hands with delight.

"Oh thank you! Thank you! I'm tired, but I'm so excited to see everyone! And I can't wait until they meet my children," she said then paused, adding mischievously, "I hope they're here to babysit so that I can get a nap."

Evelyn guffawed. "Of course. That's why I told them to come."

Evelyn let out a piercing whistle as if she were calling a cab. Mai winced at the noise, hoping that it wouldn't wake the babies, but her concerns were quickly forgotten the moment the door opened and she saw her friends. There was a round of hugs, tears, and garbled conversation where everyone spoke at once. Eventually the melee damped down and they all sat and began to catch up, one person at a time.

"What's it like?" Vanessa asked curiously, inclining her head towards the room where the dragon babies were sleeping.

Mai smiled, shrugging noncommittally.

"It's exhausting, but they're amazing. I never knew it was possible to love something so much. It's completely different from what I feel for Jake, of course, but every bit as powerful, if not more so. I can't wait to see how they grow up."

Mai paused then continued somberly. "I am worried about their future, after reading the letter my father wrote."

Vanessa furrowed her brow. "Letter? From your father? What letter?"

Mai briefly outlined the contents of the letter Astrid had given her a few short weeks earlier to general interest and silence, broken by Cat.

"That's amazing. It must have been reassuring to get it though, like your parents had given you their blessing. How crazy that the letter found you over a hundred years later. It does sound like something that was destined to be. You know, the more I see, the less in control of my life I feel. Do you guys ever feel that you're part of a bigger plan?"

Vanessa and Mai nodded, while Zahara replied with laughter.

"You guys are silly. I've never felt in control, but I guess that's likely because I grew up with Robin in my life."

Vanessa snorted. "Oh yeah, nothing like growing up with a crazy earth god for a family friend. I can see how that would contribute to a feeling of being out of control."

Evelyn smiled fondly as she listened to them speak about her man. "If I'd known even two years ago what I know now, I'd likely have done my best to stay asleep forever. Well, except for that man, of course."

Mai smiled at her. "You have the greatest responsibility with your power. I don't envy you, but I think you've been amazing. If anyone is capable of it managing it all, you are. I'm worried that my little guys will be called to do the same type of work, and when I see how it tires you out, I worry even more.

"Well, you won't have to do it alone. We'll always be here to help, whenever you need us. Are you planning on coming back to the States soon?"

Vanessa looked at Mai hopefully, looking disappointed when Mai shook her head.

"I don't think so. This feels like home now. And I want to raise my kids close to family. Plus, this is a small town where many people follow the old ways and understand and accept magic. A lot of people here have their own powers as well, while those that don't are comfortable with them the way they are. It'll be nice to not worry about discrimination, or having the kids put in a zoo by people that don't understand us."

Zahara nodded approvingly at Mai's words. "That's a good call. Growing up, we had a close community where we could be ourselves. It would have been a lot harder without that. It was hard enough being stuck next to a big city as an earth magic."

"We'll miss you, but I understand," said Vanessa. "Hopefully, you guys will visit often. Although with my career finally taking off, I should be able to afford to come out now and then."

Vanessa smiled at Mai and she smiled back. Friends forever. It was nice still having that connection, even if their friendship would have to be long distance for awhile. While Mai felt close to all of the girls, Vanessa was as close to a sister as she could imagine, and she was the one that Mai had missed the most over the months since they'd been apart.

"You better. I fully expect to still hear from you at least once a week and I'll be ticked if you don't come and see the kids at least once every few months. You're their godmother, after all."

Although not a tradition for Mai, she'd jumped at the chance to formally name the girls as protectors, based on Jake's heritage. The more protection she could give her children, the better.

"Promise." Vanessa nodded as though she was confirming a business transaction and the other girls added their assents as well.

"So, how long are you guys staying this time?" Mai asked, curious and not sure what she wanted to hear.

On one hand, she always loved to see her friends, but on the other hand, she was tired and unsure if she wanted company right now. Evelyn must have known her thoughts, because she smoothly answered before the others could.

"We've just come to say hi and give our blessing. The gate to Summerland is only open tonight, so we'll go back. But I promise we'll come back again soon."

Mai sighed, with mixture of relief and disappointment.

"Of course. Do you guys want to see the kids? We can take a peek, but I don't mind if you wake them if you have to leave right away," Mai said, then added wryly, "assuming they're sleeping, of course."

She already knew from experience that the minute she opened the door three pairs of sparkling eyes would be looking back at her, suggesting that the small demons...er, dragons, didn't actually require sleep like other creatures.

"If it's not a bother. Honestly, please don't wake them on our account," Cat protested, but Mai waved off her objections and the girls eagerly followed her to the children's room.

Inside, as expected, were three rambunctious and not at all sleepy small children. They were taking turns playing a game that involved two of the children turning into human form to ride the third one in dragon form. They stopped the moment the door opened, frozen in place and wearing guilty expressions.

Mai sighed and shook her head. "You guys are supposed to be sleeping. Naughty, naughty!"

As she'd expected, her words flew completely over their heads and they swarmed her with sticky toddler hands and scratchy dragon scales.

"Girls, these are my talented, but not very obedient, offspring. We're obviously working on basic social behaviors still."

Mai's warnings and self-deprecation went unheeded, as her friends sat on the floor to play with the children. The dragons allowed the girls to join in the game that they were inventing, with much confusion and hilarity. Mai watched with a full heart as her friends enjoyed her children, feeling as though her life had reached its full capacity in that moment.

MAI HUGGED VANESSA as they waited for the gate to open. The others had left to chat with Jake and catch up, while the two women had a private moment.

"I miss you, you know," said Vanessa, as she looked at Mai intently. "No one will ever replace you in my life, or in the kitchen. Cat's just not the homemaker that you are."

Vanessa winked, looking surreptitiously over her shoulder to where her sister stood laughing at something Jake was saying.

Mai snorted. "No kidding. I couldn't leave you to your own devices. That place was atrocious until I cleaned things up for you. And we likely wouldn't ever have had food in the house if I hadn't taken over grocery shopping. And cooking." Mai looked at Vanessa with a mock disapproval that didn't bother her friend in the slightest.

"Pshaw. I was totally fine. But I probably would've eaten out a lot more. That's true. So how long do you think until you come back?"

Mai shrugged. "I'm not sure. For now, it's all I can do to keep the kids located in the village. I'm just lucky it's a small town and that everyone's keeping an eye out for them. I found Freya trapped between the baker's and the florist's shop the other day. Thankfully, they were able to get her out and bring her home. I think I've developed three white hairs this week alone. I'm not sure when I'll feel safe bringing them anywhere and I don't think I'll ever be able to travel without them. They're my heart now. I feel actual physical pain when I'm not close to them."

Vanessa looked at her wistfully. "You look good as a mom. And Jake is amazing as a dad. You're where you guys belong. I'm so happy you found each other. I hope that I find someone as good for me as you two are for each other. And hey, maybe I'll have kids one day too." Vanessa paused. "But not too soon. I want to do a little living first. Luckily, I think my kids will come out one at a time when they do. And maybe just one in total." Vanessa looked up to the right thoughtfully, before nodding decisively. "Of course first, I need to find the right person. And that's not anytime soon, I don't think. I'm not ready yet."

Mai impulsively hugged her. "You just never know. I never thought I'd be here, and yet life has a funny way of working out when you least expect it. Make sure that you visit soon. I'll be missing you. And make sure you call often. I want to hear about your crazy Hollywood hijinks."

"You got it. Take care of the little ones."

Vanessa hugged her back and they walked over to join the others. After another round of hugs and tearful goodbyes and chasing the kids out of the Summerland gate, Mai and Jake said a last goodbye and waited until their friends had faded out of sight.

"That was short and sweet, but it was so nice to see them. Are you okay?"

Jake put down a wriggling Peter and Gaia, who promptly changed into dragons and zoomed away. Freya was still content to be held in Mai's motherly grip, but when she saw her siblings escape, she fought for release as well.

Mai shrugged and let her daughter go, watching as the three children ran off together. "It's always sad to watch them leave, but this is our life now. Honestly, it was a little strange to see them here. I think that this is the start of a new chapter for us. San Francisco feels like a lifetime ago. I'll miss them, as always, but I have everything I need here. How about you? You never got to say goodbye to your friends."

Jake smiled and shrugged his shoulders. "My guys are fine to see me now and then. We'll visit soon. And I can pick up the phone and talk to them whenever. No big."

Mai shook her head. Guys were so weird sometimes.

"Well, should we head home? It's almost time for them to eat again. And I'm really hoping they take a nap because I'm completely done with today."

"Sure, let's go. Come here, wifey."

Jake held out an arm for her to take and she did. They walked arm in arm, following behind their youngsters with a sense of contentment. They didn't know what the future would bring, but for now, they had everything.

CHAPTER
TWENTY TWO

Vanessa looked out over the San Francisco Bay. It was shrouded with fog, as it so often was. She'd enjoyed her visit with Mai, but mourned the change in their relationship. She still felt close to her emotionally, but knew that things would never be the same, considering the physical distance that was now between them. Mai was married and Jake was now her most important confidant and compatriot, not to mention the kids, who would keep them both busy for a long time to come. She thought back to their conversation about the future, wistfully considering the possibility of children of her own. She'd never seen herself as a maternal type, but damn, Mai's kids had made her wonder what it would be like.

She was glad that Cat had taken over Mai's room when she'd left. It would have been harder to be alone after having a roommate. They got along well most of the time, for sisters, anyway. And she had other friends, but none she was as close to as Mai. No one who understood the other side of life that most people couldn't see or understand. She stood up, turning away from the view and walking back the path to home.

It felt odd to be so sad when everything was going well and she hoped that the feeling would soon pass. It was hard for Vanessa, with her emotional and sometimes impulsive nature, to stay calm when she felt adrift. She felt a breeze start to pick up and forced herself to stay even. It had become easier to make herself relax with practice, but sometimes her emotions still could make the weather around her unpredictable.

A sudden prickling on her neck caused her to shiver and she stopped walking. Looking around, she couldn't see anything on the path ahead, so she turned her neck to look behind her. The light from the park lamp was muted, but bright enough to see that there was nothing there. Uneasy, she turned around and called her power to her, ready in case of a fight, and picked up the pace.

Seeing the edge of the park appear in front of her, she felt her heart rate begin to return to normal until a figure stepped into her path, causing it to speed up again. Cursing her inability to read people the way Cat or Evelyn could, she kept walking, giving the person ahead room to get by on the path in the hope that they'd continue walking past her.

"Vanessa?"

A throaty voice as rich as caramel came from a figure that was still obscured by fog and the night, but Vanessa could see the person was wearing dark glasses and had a white cane tapping on the path in front of them.

A blind person? Vanessa felt calm wash over her as the prickling settled, as though it had been smoothed down by a warm hand.

"Yes? Who are you?" Vanessa asked the now visible person, who stood only a few feet away.

Vanessa watched as the woman stopped and tilted her head slightly to the side. Shiny dark brown hair fell in a sheet over one shoulder down the length of her arm and a small smile curved deep red lips. The dark glasses hid her eyes. Vanessa found herself curious regarding what colour they were underneath.

"A mutual friend told me where to find you. We have much to discuss and we must talk soon. You are not safe."

Vanessa scowled, irritated by the idea of more danger. "Says who? Which friend are you talking about? And you still haven't told me your name."

The woman bowed her head in acknowledgement. "My apologies. Names have power, you see, and I prefer not to speak mine in the open, in case unfriendly ears are nearby. Evelyn sent me and said we'd be able to help each other. She's had a dream, you see."

Vanessa felt her misgivings fade slightly. It felt like the truth. She also knew that Cat was waiting at home, so the safest place to talk would be there, even with taking the chance of inviting a stranger into their apartment.

"Well, I guess you should come with me then. We can talk inside, where it's safer."

The woman smiled, and tipped her head slightly in acknowledgement.

"I shall follow you there."

Vanessa sighed, and continued walking along the path with the feeling that big things were about to change in her life, but not yet knowing what that change would entail.

ALSO BY H. M. GOODEN

Look for more news on upcoming adventures on H. M. Gooden's site, www.hmgoodenauthor.com or any of her other social media links;

twitter- https://twitter.com/HMGoodenauthor

email at- books@hmgoodenauthor.com

facebook page- https://www.facebook.com/.../.../author/show/17229510.H_M_Gooden

facebook fan page - Summerland Gate

https://www.facebook.com/groups/981341802029808/?ref=bookmarks

Bookbub-   https://www.bookbub.com/profile/h-m-gooden

Instagram-   https://www.instagram.com/hmgoodenauthor/

Goodreads- 17229510.H_M_Gooden

COPYRIGHT INFORMATION

and do not participate in or encourage electronic piracy of copyrighted materials.

Published in Canada by H. M. Gooden.
www.Hmgoodenauthor.com.

NOTE FROM THE AUTHOR

Thank you so much for taking the time to read my book! I hope you've enjoyed reading about the adventures of my characters as much as I enjoy writing them. I'd initially started my series with the intention to write just one book, then it turned into a trilogy, and then I created my own world. (I have issues with goodbye, apparently!)

Reader reviews are incredibly important to indie authors like myself, so it would mean so much if you could take a few minutes to leave an honest review wherever you buy books online. Even a few words can make the difference in helping a future reader give a book a chance, as every review makes a novel more visible in the vast ocean of literature.

If you're interested in receiving updates, giveaways, or advanced copies of upcoming books, sign up for my mailing list at books@hmgoodenauthor.com, or through my webpage at www.hmgoodenauthor.com. You can also follow me on Facebook, Instagram, Twitter and many other places. I always love to hear from readers and do my best to answer every comment when possible. I hope you will join me in my next adventure!

Did you love *Dragons are Forever*? Then you should read *The Stone Dragon* by H. M. Gooden!

Cat has finally settled into her new town and is happy with life just the way it is. Until the day that her friend Evelyn shows up on her front step, with a recurring nightmare that began after they defeated Declan.A dark stranger surrounded by fire and destruction tortures her every night, and in order to help her, Cat must discover the truth about the dark man and his origins.This time, they must face a much older evil on new ground. With the addition of a new ally, the girls will stand against darkness together. Will they be victorious, or will they fall to his power the same way so many others have?

Read more at https://www.facebook.com/HMGoode-nauthor/.

About the Author

H. M. Gooden has always loved the world of books, but over the last few years a new story has begged to be told, and as a result, this series was born.In between dealing with children and work, the majority of the actual writing happens between four and six am and involves multiple cups of coffee for inspiration.You can always find me @HMGoodenauthor on twitter, where I'm likely spending more time than I should, or on my facebook page, or at HMGoodenauthor.com.I always love to hear from readers!

Read more at https://www.facebook.com/HMGoodenauthor/.